Judge Dredd

The Junior Novelisation

Judge Dredd

The Junior Novelisation

by
Graham Marks

Based on the screenplay by
William Wisher
and
Steven E. de Souza

BOXTREE

First published in the UK 1995 by Boxtree Limited
Broadwall House, 21 Broadwall, London SE1 9PL.

10 9 8 7 6 5 4 3 2 1

Typeset in Century by SX Composing Ltd, Rayleigh, Essex
Printed and bound in Great Britain by
Cox & Wyman, Reading, Berkshire

A catalogue record for this book is available from
the British Library

ISBN: 0 7522 0671 0

Chapter 1

In the Third Millennium, the world changed.

Climate. Politics. Nations. All were in upheaval.

Humanity itself turned as violent as the planet and civilisation threatened to collapse. And then a solution was found.

The teeth of the legal system were combined with the claws of the police to create a strong and efficient single force. These new guardians of what was left of Society became all-powerful. They were the law, the jury and the executioner, all in one. They were ...

The Judges!

The Aspen Prison Shuttle came out of the violent orange sunset as it dragged darkness across the Cursed Earth. Skimming across the deadlands where nothing grew – and nothing would, ever again – the shuttle's retro jets fired as it approached the walls of Mega City 1.

In the year 2139 this was one of the few places on Earth where you could live. If you could call it living.

'Shuttle No. 3 docking!' a voice rasped out of the

loudspeakers in the air lock. 'Commence anti-contam-ination – spray *all* released prisoners before they disembark!'

'You sometimes wonder why they want to come back here,' said one of the waiting guards as the air lock hissed open.

'If you'd been to Aspen you'd know,' replied another guard, eyes narrowing as the first of the ex-perps appeared.

They were a sad, grey lot. Blinking in the harsh lights, they shuffled forward in a ragged line, each having his name called and ticked off on a list as they made their way towards the waiting taxi shuttle that would take them back into the Big Meg.

'Ferguson, Herman!' barked the guard doing the checking.

'Yes?' said a confused-looking man.

'That's "Yes *sir*!", Ferguson,' said the guard.

'Yes, sir,' repeated Herman 'Fergie' Ferguson.

'Sent to Aspen for computer-related offences, six months of sentence served,' the guard read from the list in front of him. 'You wanna hack, you cough in-stead, Ferguson. Put one foot wrong and you'll be back inside so fast your feet won't touch the street.'

'Er, sure,' mumbled Fergie.

'So, welcome back, Citizen!' the guard almost smiled. 'Your living quarters will be in Block Y, Heavenly Haven, Red Quad. Next!'

'Heavenly Haven,' thought Fergie, 'sounds nice . . .'

Mega City 1. An amazing combination of the best and

the worst of the modern world. Towering steel and glass buildings, graceful skyways, the air punctuated by flying traffic. Filthy sewers, congested walkways, decaying tenement buildings, the air filled with pollution and the cries of angry Citizens.

'I don't believe it!' yelled a tired Heavenly Haven resident, pointing at a massive vid poster. 'They've stolen our park!'

The vid poster, which had been promising the rezzies a new Pocket Park, now told the growing crowd that, instead, they were getting a brand new Law Enforcement Barracks. The Judges had lied.

From the window of a scummy apartment in Red Quad – home to a band of illegal squatters – Zed, their leader, looked down at what appeared to be the start of a brand new riot.

'They're going mental out there!' Twist turned to the four other creeps in the room. There was a mad look in his eyes. 'What d'you say, Zed?'

'I say let's give 'em a hand!' Zed nodded to the one called Reggie. 'Wake up the guns, Reggie-boy!'

Reggie smiled and lifted up the mattress he was sitting on. Hidden underneath it was a collection of the meanest-looking weapons outside of the Judges' armoury.

The taxi shuttle flew past skycars and buses, weaving between beautiful high-rise buildings with roof-top swimming pools. The smog gave the air a weird yellow tinge.

'Is one of these Heavenly Haven?' asked Fergie.

'No such luck,' grinned the pilot, taking the shuttle down. The nearer the ground the older and filthier the buildings got, until the taxi landed in a rubbish-filled street.

'Here you go,' said the pilot, opening the door.

'Still, better than Aspen,' muttered Fergie as he got out. Then, and as the taxi took off again, a brick sailed over his head and bounced down the street. 'Maybe . . .'

In the distance he could hear raised voices shouting. It sounded something like 'Block war! Block war!', and in the gloom he could see a surging mass of people coming towards him. A couple of bottles smashed on the ground nearby.

'Time to get off the street,' said Fergie, running for the doorway with a sign saying 'Red Quad' above it.

He dodged through dingy corridors and up litter-strewn stairs, unnoticed by the people making their way outside to join the riot. Reaching what he thought was the right floor, Fergie stopped to check his papers in the dim light.

'Delicious and healthful ration packs!' twittered a robot Food Cart as it came down the passage towards him. 'Piping hot and ready to eat!'

'Later,' mumbled Fergie, 'when I've settled in.'

It was then that he spotted the door to what the papers said was his apartment. It was open. Curious, but cautious, Fergie poked his head round to look inside. He found himself staring down the barrel of a gun.

'What do we have here?' cackled Zed. 'You a Judge spy, little man?'

8

'No!' Fergie shook his head. He could hear other people laughing, but he didn't dare look away from the gun. 'Look, I've got papers to say I live here!'

'That so?' said Zed.

'But I'm sure I don't mind going to stay in a hotel, guys!'

'No way, man!' said Twist, pulling Fergie into the apartment and closing the door. 'There's a block war out there, man! Rezzies gotta stick up for their blocks, right?'

'But I'm on parole, guys – if I get into any trouble I'll be back in Aspen . . .' Zed stuck his gun in Fergie's cheek; '. . . but who cares when your block needs you, right? Let's go Haven!'

A worried look on his face, Fergie watched Zed go the apartment window and look out. Sounds of the riot drifted up from below. Suddenly Zed yelled 'BLOCK WAR!!' and began spraying the street with bullets.

'Did you see that?' Zed yelled. 'I'm making them dance down there!'

This was the signal for the rest of the squatters to join in, letting loose with everything they had; high-powered weaponry opened up from every room, the peppery smell of cordite filling the air as empty shell cases leapt out of stuttering automatics and skittered across the floor like heavy metal ants.

Rezzies from the opposite block, not wanting to be left out of the fun, began firing back; the plasterwork of Fergie's new home got some extra design features, as the walls exploded under the impact of hundreds of mercury-tipped lead slugs.

9

'Welcome to the neighbourhood,' sighed Fergie.

The Law can't be everywhere, all the time, but in Mega City 1 it can get to where it's needed so fast it almost doesn't matter. Word of the riot at Heavenly Haven had got through to Judge Hershey and Judge Brisco, out on the street riding their massive Lawmaster bikes.

These machines were like mobile gun platforms, their riders able to dispense justice at the touch of a button. Under normal circumstances perps and criminals ran at the sight of them, but in a riot normal circumstances don't exist.

As the two Judges powered up the streets, guns that had been aimed at rival block members turned on the hated figures of authority, spraying them with a hail of bullets.

'Just like an Academy simulation,' grinned Judge Brisco, 'right down to the crossfire – I'll lead, you follow!'

'This is no simulation, Brisco – this is the real thing!' Hershey grabbed the rookie Judge and yanked him back behind his bike. 'Stand down, you idiot! We got to wait for back up!'

Hershey spoke into her helmet mike: 'We're in position outside Heavenly Haven, control . . . under heavy fire from upper floors, particularly Level Y – repeat Y – request back up, nearest Judge!'

Pinned down by the barrage of fire, Hershey and Brisco could do nothing but wait. Any other course of action could prove fatal. Smoke filled the street, automatic weapons fire tore the air apart and tortured screams echoed off the block walls. It was hell out there.

Hershey tried to squeeze off a couple of shots, but was forced back behind her bike by ricocheting bullets. Somewhere in the distance she could hear the unmistakable sound of a Lawmaster and seconds later it was there, whipping round the corner of the nearest block.

From where they were it was impossible to see who was riding the bike, and then a Molotov Cocktail sailed out of an upper floor, exploding on the tarmac. A slick sheet of orange flame billowed skywards and the Lawmaster disappeared from view.

'Did they get him?' asked Brisco.

'I don't think so,' replied Hershey, as the flames parted like curtains and let the bike through. It stopped in the middle of the rising chaos and the rider got off.

'Who the heck's that?' spluttered Brisco. 'He's a sitting duck out there – he's gonna . . .'

'Sit back and pay attention, kid,' said Hershey, relaxing. 'This guy knows what he's doing.'

Chapter 2

Six feet of armoured justice stepped out of the flames and stood stock still, looking round, observing a world gone mad. Raised at the Academy, this man knew what duty and honour meant, he understood what it was to be Judge, Jury and Executioner. It was in his blood.

'Dredd . . .?' whispered Brisco.

'The very same,' replied Hershey.

'Grud!' said Brisco, watching as Judge Dredd picked up the speaker-phone from his Lawmaster.

'Drop your weapons, Citizens!' growled Dredd, his words thudding like hammer blows off the scarred block walls. 'You're all under arrest!'

If anyone else in Mega City 1 had uttered these words, the reply would have come in a full metal jacket. But this wasn't just anyone, and silence fell like an air-tight lid.

In the apartment on Level Y everyone looked at Zed.

'It's Judge Dredd!' whined Twist, moving away from the window.

'So?' Zed grabbed a bag of ammunition and reloaded his gun.

'But ... Dredd!'

'You gonna be scared of anyone in this little old world, Twist, you should be scared of me!' Zed pushed Twist out of his way and went to the window.

'How about I go out there and throw him off his guard by surrendering?' said Fergie.

'How about you shut up and keep them magazines loaded like I told you,' yelled Zed, pushing the barrel of his gun out of the window and firing off a burst. 'Come and get us, Dreddy!'

With Zed showing them the only way to go, everyone else in the room began unloading bullet clips at the street once more. In a riot zone silence never lasts for long.

Lead rain fell on to the ground, spanking off the pavement as Dredd walked slowly over to the waiting Judges.

'20mm caseless flechet rounds at six hundred feet,' muttered Dredd as he joined his companions. 'Effective lethal range is thirteen metres. We're safe ... What gives, Hershey?'

'We were waiting for back up.'

'It's here,' said Dredd, 'so let's go. Keep it simple, standard relay, single file – I'm point.'

Hershey nodded, and as she did so Brisco, eager to prove himself in battle, moved off in front.

'You,' Dredd stopped him. 'You're last.'

Giving instructions to his voice-activated Lawgiver gun, Dredd blew the doors off the block entrance with a grenade. Stepping over the smoking debris, the three Judges entered the building one after the other.

'They're on the 48th,' Dredd spoke grimly. 'Meet me there.'

'We splitting up?' said Hershey, confused. 'What're you gonna do?'

But there was no answer to the question. Fire shadows danced in the corridor where Dredd had been standing.

Things were getting really out of hand, thought Fergie as he passed yet more ammo clips to Zed, Twist and the others. How could life be so unfair? First he gets thrown in jail for a harmless bit of computer hacking, then he gets let out on parole, only to find himself reloading guns for a bunch of psychos with a death wish. And on his way to make that wish come true was the biggest, baddest, meanest Judge ever to earn his badge.

It was with that thought worrying him that Fergie heard the whirr of an electric motor out in the hallway; a digitised voice was asking if anyone wanted any delicious and healthful ration packs. A much less worrying thought then occurred to Fergie.

By now it was hard to see or hear anything in the trashed apartment on the 48th floor of Red Quad. The only light came from the flames licking hungrily at the blitzed living quarters in the opposite block.

There was a madness in the air, a kill-frenzy of epic proportions. Guns bucked in the hands of Reggie, Zed and the rest, their faces twisted, their teeth bared, deaf and blind to everything except mayhem. None of them saw or heard what was happening above them as a circle of holes appeared in the ceiling.

An explosion of dust rolled through the room as a section of ceiling fell to the floor. Crouched on it was Judge Dredd, a gun blazing in each hand.

'This room is pacified!' he growled, his shots catching two of the squatters by surprise. As their lifeless bodies hit the floor Dredd stomped over to the next room. But before he could get there Judge Brisco burst through from the passageway, Hershey right behind him.

'This one's mine!' he yelled.

'No!' screamed Hershey.

But her warning came too late. Brisco found himself face to face with Twist, Reggie and Zed. All three opened fire at once, blowing the young Judge backwards off his feet, his Lawgiver falling out of his hand and into the room.

'Stupid ... stupid ...' moaned Brisco, as Hershey pulled his dying body out of the way.

Inside the room Twist saw the Lawgiver lying on the floor. It looked awesome. He could see there were just two Judges left, but two Judges were like an army. They needed an edge. He reached out to pick up the Lawgiver. Now that's what you called an edge.

'You're all under arrest,' Dredd shouted. 'Surrender now, or prepare to receive your sentences!'

Seconds ticked by. Twist picked up the gun.

'Don't!' whispered Zed. 'It's booby-trapped!'

Dredd spoke to his Lawgiver: 'Full auto. Rapid fire,' he said.

Twist ignored Zed and aimed at the doorway. 'Come and get it, Judges!' he crowed, pulling the trigger.

For a moment nothing happened. The gun seemed to be thinking. Then, with a huge surge of power, it sent a bolt of electricity zapping through Twist's body. As the squatter writhed on the floor, Dredd dived through the doorway and raked the room with auto-fire.

Reggie and Zed opened up with a blistering reply, but it was hardly worth the effort.

'Armour-piercing,' ordered Dredd.

One of Reggie's massive guns disintegrated, but he and Zed still charged Dredd.

'Double whammy,' Dredd instructed his Lawgiver.

Two bullets were fired at once, each finding its target. Both men were punched to the ground, their weapons flying out of their hands.

'Mega City Municipal Code 334.8.' Dredd stood over Zed, informing the man of the charges levelled against him. It had to be done, it was The Law. 'Wilful destruction of property – two years.'

Zed pushed himself away from the Judge. Reggie made a grab for his gun and Hershey's Lawgiver barked a lethal round into his chest.

'Code 11-5C: resisting arrest – five years,' Dredd continued.

Zed's hand brushed against something behind him as he stood up by one of the windows.

'Code 34-A: resisting arrest – twenty years.'

Zed whipped the gun round.

'9804: assault on a Judge with deadly intent,' Dredd looked at the blood-soaked man.

'Don't tell me,' Zed grinned crazily. 'Life.'

'No.' Dredd fired his Lawgiver. 'Death.'

Zed crashed backwards through the open window, his scream fading away.

'Court adjourned.' Dredd put away his gun.

The corridor outside what was supposed to have been Fergie's new home was now full of Judges and paramedics, although there was little left for them to do.

'I was supposed to watch out for him, dammit!' said Hershey.

'Don't blame yourself.' Dredd looked over and saw two paramedics pick up the stretcher with Brisco's body on it. 'He made the mistake, not you. Fill in a Negative Report, Hershey . . . his reactions were slow, judgement faulty.'

'That'll make me feel a whole lot better, Dredd!' Hershey scowled. 'How about being allowed to have emotions once in a while?'

But Dredd wasn't listening to his colleague. Something had caught his attention, one sound among so many noises, so much confusion. Making its way slowly down the corridor, dodging bodies and debris, came a robot Food Cart. There was something odd about the way it moved, and, frowning, Dredd walked in front of it.

'Halt!' he said. 'You have ten seconds to surrender . . . nine . . . eight . . .'

17

'Healthful and nutritious food rations, ready to eat!' said the Food Cart.

'It's just a service-droid,' said Hershey, hardly believing what she was seeing – had Dredd gone mad?

'Make your selection and insert your credit in the slot!' said the Food Cart.

Dredd unholstered his Lawgiver and jabbed the muzzle in the credit slot. '. . . three . . . two . . .'

'I give up,' said Fergie, uncoiling himself from the cramped interior of the Food Cart, his hands still full of the wires he'd been using to control it. 'Don't shoot.'

'Mega City Municipal Code 1286.4: wilful sabotage of a public droid – that's six months, Citizen. Let's see your Unicard.'

'Gimme a break, Judge . . .' Fergie peered at Dredd's badge, saw the name and promptly fainted. Hershey took the Unicard out of his limp hand and ran her scanner over it.

'Ferguson, Herman,' she read off the display. 'Hacker . . . illegal tampering with City computers and credit machines . . . small time . . .'

'He hasn't even been out of jail for a day and look what he's up to,' sneered Dredd, looking at Fergie as he got up off the floor. 'A habitual criminal, Hershey. That's an automatic five-year sentence.'

'Five years!' wailed Fergie. 'But I had no choice, Judge – they woulda trashed me!'

'You could have gone out the window, Ferguson.' Dredd turned away.

'Forty-eight floors?!' spluttered Fergie. 'That woulda been suicide!'

18

'Maybe, but it would've been legal,' Dredd walked off. 'And now you got five years in Aspen Prison Facility to look forward, Ferguson. Case closed, take him away.'

'He might've been telling the truth,' said Hershey as Fergie was dragged away. 'Never heard of having a reasonable excuse?'

'I've heard it all, Hershey.' Dredd sounded bored. 'And it never makes a blind bit of difference.'

Chapter 3

Looking like the symbol of the Judge System itelf, the eagle-shaped Hall of Justice was the gleaming heart of Mega City 1, a heart of stone. For it was within these towering walls that Justice lived and breathed. From its doors walked the men and women who were the Law, and in its mighty Central Chamber sat the Council of Judges.

They were in full session, seated round a vast black table in the centre of which was a map of North America. Apart from the sites of Mega Cities 1 and 2 (what had been New York and Los Angeles), and Texas City (old Houston), the rest was a dark limbo called the Cursed Earth.

In the throne-like chair set higher than the rest sat Chief Justice Fargo, listening intently to the words of Judge Griffin.

'My fellow Justices,' said Griffin, 'have we forgotten the lessons of history? However quickly these block wars can be dealt with, it's clear they are not going to go away that easily. They're a disease that must cured immediately . . . and the only solution is a tougher Criminal Code!'

The Council Chamber erupted in a storm of noise

as the assembled Judges reacted to Griffin's words.

'Seventy-three riots in sixteen different sectors in the last two months!' yelled a short-tempered Judge Silver.

'If we don't increase our resources,' said Judge McGruder, slamming her hand on the table, 'they'll be inadequate in under three years!'

'Three years?' laughed Judge Esposito. 'They're inadequate now!'

A sharp crack, almost like a pistol shot, rang out in the Council Chamber and the shouting ceased.

'My fellow Council Members.' Chief Justice Fargo put his metal gavel back on the table. 'We must remember that, as a city, we continue to grow. And growth is always painful. *Sixty-five million* people live in an area built to take under twenty million people – that's over 200% more than sanity should allow ... and they all need clothes, food, water and justice ...'

'Chief,' interrupted Griffin, 'Mega City is in chaos, we need more Law and less social conscience – my curfew proposals should be put into practice straight away!'

'Treat men like animals,' sighed Fargo, 'and they'll repay you by acting like animals; it's a simple but honest truth.'

'Perhaps you'd prefer we strip the Judges of their current powers and return to the old system of trial by jury?' sneered Griffin. 'Prison hasn't worked – it's no deterrent – and I say we start executing offenders for lesser crimes!'

'This Council is not the first assembly to think that more laws, and fewer choices, will bring peace and order ... that solution has been tried before and found to be no solution at all.' Chief Justice Fargo looked pointedly at Griffin, then continued: 'My fellow Judges, I was a young teenager when I first put on my badge, and when the time comes for me to finally take it off I want to do it knowing it stood for freedom ... and not fear.'

The Council Chamber was silent as the assembled Judges thought about what what Fargo had said.

'Once again, Chief Justice, you have made your point extremely well,' said Judge Griffin, sitting back in his chair. He could tell the mood in the Chamber had changed. 'I'm sure we all agree with you, and I withdraw my proposals – I hope for good.'

With the meeting over the Council broke up, the Judges leaving to carry on with their work. As Griffin came out into the corridor he saw Dredd standing by a TV monitor that showed a news broadcast. The reporter, Vardis Hammond, stood in front of Heavenly Haven and behind him workers were clearing up after the riot.

'... fifty-three people have been hospitalised, five of them children,' Vardis was saying, 'nineteen residents are dead, four allegedly killed by a gang of squatters who were themselves killed, in what this reporter would call a high-handed, dictatorial fashion, by Judge Dredd.'

'Grud!' spat Dredd. 'A rookie Judge died there today too, cut down like an animal by an animal . . . I guess he wasn't worth mentioning.'

'I guess not,' Griffin smiled wryly, 'that might confuse the viewers; after all, we can't be the victims, Dredd – we're already the villains.'

'Things will change, sir.'

'Every night I pray it will happen,' said Griffin, walking off down the corridor.

Dredd turned back to the monitor, where Vardis Hammond's face was now filling the screen. 'Some say that working these mean streets, day after day, makes killing machines out of the Judges – but is it the streets or the Judges themselves that have created this atmosphere of savagery?' he asked his millions of viewers. 'As my special undercover report continues tomorrow night, I'll take you behind the walls of the Hall of Justice for a disturbing probe into the recent upsurge in riots and block wars – are they a coincidence, or are they deliberate?'

'Dredd!' boomed a voice from behind him. He turned to see Chief Justice Fargo standing at the door to the Council Chamber, beckoning him. With a last glance at the monitor, Dredd turned and went into the empty cathedral-like room.

'Yes, Chief Judge?' he said.

'Joseph,' sighed Fargo, looking up at the pictorial history on the wall – a reminder of the wars, famines and violence that had destroyed the world. 'Joseph, you know I've always taken a special interest in your career . . .'

'I appreciate it, sir.'

'So, tell me, Joseph ... seven "high-handed and dictatorial executions", to quote Mr Hammond – were they, um, necessary?'

'Unavoidable, sir.'

'Unavoidable?' frowned the Chief Judge. 'We are not pawns in this chess game, Joseph – we are Judges ... we make the rules.'

'With all due respect, sir, times have changed.' Dredd looked straight at the older man. 'Life doesn't mean much out there any more ... you'd know that if you weren't...' Dredd hesitated.

'Go on, Joseph – you were never one to pull your punches.'

'If you weren't always at the Academy, sir.'

'Don't you mean, always at the Academy, molly-coddling Cadets?' said Fargo. 'Isn't that what they're saying in the squad room?'

'It doesn't matter what they say in the squad room, sir,' frowned Dredd. 'It's what happens on the streets that counts, and you set the standards there.'

'I may set the standards, but you put them into practice, Joseph,' Fargo sat down in his chair. 'You're a legend in the Hall of Justice, from the bottom to the top.'

'Sir?'

'You command respect, Joseph ... you were my finest student. I want you to go back to the Academy – from tomorrow you're going to spend two days a week there, teaching.'

24

'I'd be honoured,' Dredd shifted on his feet. 'Teaching what – unarmed combat? Marksmanship?'

'Ethics, morals, principles and standards,' said Chief Justice Fargo. 'You should *all* learn something.'

Chapter 4

If the Cursed Earth is hell on Earth, then Aspen Prison Facility is hell's jail. Outside the mountain fortress there are ceaseless violent blizzards. Inside, conditions aren't much better. "Grim" would be a kind way of describing them.

Aspen's warden, Judge Miller, strode through the gruesome, forbidding complex, two armed guards at his heels. Past row upon row of cramped steel isocubes they went, down through increasingly dirty and crumbling levels until they reached a massive nickel-chromag door.

Miller put his right hand on to the computer-controlled access pad and waited. A red light eventually turned green and there was a muffled click. A huge pair of servo motors began to whine as the door slowly opened on the highest security cube anywhere in the world.

The warden stepped alone into the room, watching as autoguns, mounted high on the walls, swung round to point at him.

'Remain still,' the guns' controlling synth-chip ordered. 'Identify yourself.'

'Miller, warden,' said the Judge, sweating slightly. He hated being ordered around by computers.

'Voice sample recognised,' came the reply. 'Thank you, warden.'

The pair of guns swung back to join the others pointing at the circular platform, ringed by blue light, at the edge of the circular steel room. Behind the light Miller could make out a figure as it moved around.

'Warden,' said the ghostly shadow, 'have you come for another chat?'

'Only a short one, Rico,' said Miller. 'Duty calls me elsewhere, I'm afraid.'

'You look tired, Miller.' The figure stopped pacing. 'You must loathe this job – spending public money on looking after worthless perps.'

'Especially you, Rico.'

'I don't cost the taxpayer anything, Miller,' said Rico, moving into the light. 'I don't exist.'

'I wish,' said Judge Warden Miller.

'We're both prisoners here – you as much as me,' grinned Rico. 'Some reward Fargo gave you for being so loyal!'

'I do my job,' snarled Miller. 'You made a mockery of your badge by killing innocent people!'

'*Innocent?*' sneered Rico. 'Get real, Miller – the only difference between guilt and innocence is down to whether you get caught!'

'Oh, really?'

'Yeah, really, Miller,' said Rico. 'The same rules apply to everyone, even you. When did you become guilty – when you agreed to let me live, or when you took the bribes to keep me alive?'

'Shut it, Rico!' Miller didn't appreciate being reminded of his nasty little secret. 'Just feel grateful you've got air in your lungs, even if it is reprocessed.'

'So why're you here, Miller?' asked Rico.

'Got a package from the mystery man who's looking out for you.' Miller looked up at the ceiling. 'De-activate shield, autoguns only.'

The blue light faded, revealing a slim, fit-looking man. A man with the light of true madness in his eyes. Even the autoguns seemed nervous, edgily following his every move.

The warden stepped up on to the platform and gave Rico a small, flat package. Taking it, he put his thumb on the lock, which clicked and opened; inside Miller caught a glimpse of Rico's old Judge's badge and frowned. What was going on? Miller watched as Rico took a tiny cylinder and a photograph – which appeared to be of that mouthy newsman Vardis Hammond – out of the package.

'What's that?' he asked, pointing at the cylinder. From where he stood it looked to be some kind of game.

'It's an ancient puzzle,' grinned Rico. 'Solving it gives you the meaning of Life!'

'Nice idea, something for you to play with on these cold winter nights,' said Miller sarcastically. 'So tell me, Rico – what is the meaning of Life?'

'It ends,' said Rico, his eyes narrowing as he pointed the "puzzle" at Miller's throat, and fired.

'*Com ... pu ... ter!*' wheezed Miller, a hand gripping his bloody throat. '*Acti ... vate a ... larm!*'

'Alien voice sample,' said the synth-chip. 'Not recognised – remain still!'

The pain made it hard for Miller to think straight, but two things were crystal clear. First: some maniac had sent Rico a weapon, which was bad enough, and second: if the synth-chip didn't recognise his voice he was in even more trouble, if such a thing was possible. He had to get to the door and alert the two guards outside.

Miller flung himself off the platform.

'Security breach,' the synth-chip sounded quite calm. 'Autoguns, zero on moving target.'

Miller had no chance. He was dead before his body hit the ground.

Outside the cube the two guards heard the soft rattle of gunfire. Riot guns fully armed, they readied themselves by the door and one of them punched the override code in the access terminal to open the lock and turn off the autoguns. As the servo motors heaved tons of metal on its hinges, they charged inside.

'One down – where's the other?' said the first guard, staring down at Miller's body.

'Can't get the staff these days!' said Rico, leaping on to the second guard and breaking his neck in one quick twist. 'Didn't they teach you to always cover your back?'

As the first guard turned, all he saw was Rico scooping up his fallen comrade's weapon. A second later he had a neat hole right between his eyes.

'Whaddaya know!' grinned Rico. 'I'm back!'

The indoor training area at the Academy rang with almost continuous bursts of automatic fire. One man, surrounded by a group of Cadets, was demonstrating the fine art of survival in the modern world.

'Kevlar-9,' Dredd told his students, who watched with silent awe as bullets ricocheted off the dummy target. 'Helmet and body armour – yours when you graduate . . . *if* you graduate.'

Leaving the firing range, Dredd moved on to another section where a tech was waiting to give him a brand new gun, its oiled surfaces gleaming dully.

'Lawgiver II,' explained Dredd. 'A twenty-five round sidearm with mission-variable voice-programmed ammunition. Which means, if I say . . .' he spoke directly at the gun, '. . . signal flare . . .'

Dredd pulled the trigger and an achingly bright globe of light exploded in the air above him. There was a sharp intake of breath from the Cadets.

'Yours, when you graduate,' Dredd repeated, taking his students on down the line to the next demonstration.

'And here we have the Mark IV Lawmaster,' Dredd pointed at the latest version of the hi-tech iron horse that every Judge rode. 'This now has on-board dual laser cannons, vertical take off and landing – plus advanced flight capabilities – and a 500km range. Show them,' Dredd told the techs.

Using a remote control unit, one of the techs fired the bike's engine and retracted its wheels. The bike hovered above the ground, steady as a rock. And then some circuitry blew, sparks arcing from underneath a side panel, and the engine coughed and died.

'Yours,' said Dredd as the wheels silently folded out again and the bike settled on the floor, 'if they ever get the thing to work.'

From another part of the training area Judge Hershey watched Dredd walk over to a desk and turn to face his students.

'All of these things are nothing but toys,' she heard him say. 'At the end of the day, when you're alone in the dark, all that really counts is – this!'

Hershey saw Dredd pick something up off the table and let it drop with a meaningful thud.

'This is the Law!' growled Dredd, pointing at the book in front of him. 'And never forget, you *will* be alone when you swear to live by its rules.'

The Cadets shuffled nervously. They hadn't been expecting the legendary Judge Dredd to give them such a downbeat message; neither had Hershey, who frowned as she listened to her colleague's final words.

'For most of us there is only death on the streets,' he continued. 'Or, for those lucky enough to survive, the proud loneliness of the Long Walk, when we can spend our last days taking Justice and the Law into the Cursed Earth. And that is as good as it gets – class dismissed . . .'

Some time later, as Hershey was towelling her hair dry after a work-out and a shower, she was approached by a short, determined Cadet called

31

Olmeyer. He was carrying a large book under one arm.

'Forget it, Olmeyer,' said Hershey. 'I am *not* going to be the Cadet Yearbook centrefold, and that's final!'

'It's not a centrefold, it's a *calendar*!' beamed Olmeyer. 'It won't be a tacky 3D hologram, honest – this year's edition's going to be a classic, real old-fashioned 2D printing and everything! Here, let me show you . . .'

'When are you going to learn to take no for an answer, Olmeyer?' said Hershey, pushing the Cadet out of her way and walking off. 'Because if you don't, you'll end up with an old-fashioned 2D face!'

Followed by the sound of a group of his friends sniggering by the door, Olmeyer left the locker room with as much dignity as he could manage. Hershey turned to finish getting changed and caught sight of Judge Dredd. He'd taken off his helmet and looked very thoughtful; Hershey went over to him.

'I caught your lecture today,' she said. 'Is that what you *really* think the Cadets need to hear?'

Dredd didn't answer for a long moment. 'I told them the truth,' he said finally.

'Well, your truth, maybe,' replied Hershey. 'But you made it sound as if our lives were practically over already.'

'Parts are, Hershey.'

'What about our personal lives?' said Hershey. 'I have relations, friends . . .'

'And when did you last see any of them?' interrupted Dredd.

'My shifts keep changing,' Hershey frowned, 'it's hard to stay in touch . . .'

'You haven't been on the street for as long as I have.' Dredd turned to his locker. 'You still think it's going to get better.'

'It will!' exclaimed Hershey.

'I'm here to tell you it doesn't.' Dredd took off his armoured jacket, and Hershey could see that his finely-muscled body was criss-crossed with scars.

'You're wrong, Dredd . . . no one's supposed to alone all the time . . . don't you have any friends?' she asked.

'I had one,' Dredd replied. 'Once.'

'And?'

'And I had to judge him,' replied Dredd, the tone of his voice sending a shiver down Hershey's back.

In the dead of night, commonly known as the Graveyard Shift, a shuttle from the Aspen Prison Facility lay shrouded in gloom in a docking bay. It was on a cargo run and there was very little security.

'So,' said a guard, 'whatya got for me tonight?'

'Two loads from the prison factory in Hold 1, metal ore in Holds 3 and 4,' the shuttle crew member checked items off on his hand-held computer, 'and finally, in-coming prisoner mail in Hold 2.'

'No prisoners?'

'Just dead ones.' The crewman pointed to a row of clear plastic body bags as he went back into the shuttle. 'Bet their families are gonna be real glad to see them again.'

'Yeah,' said the guard, nodding to himself as the airlock door closed. 'Now they gotta bury them.'

Behind him one of the body bags sat up, the plastic creaking loudly. The guard turned, puzzled by the noise, but he was too late. A needle-point of laser light shot out of the bag and hit his forehead.

'Bull's eye!' grinned Rico, as he unzipped the body bag.

Chapter 5

In any city there are the good parts of town and there are the bad parts, and the Big Meg was no different. Down where crime is not just a way of life, it's the *only* way of life, the future isn't slick and shiny – it's dangerous and evil. Just the way Rico liked it.

His eyes flicked left and right, taking in the crowded streets, the bright lights of packed bars and scuzzy amusement arcades, the sheer wonderfulness of all the noise, dirt and criminal energy! This is what he'd missed most, caged like a wild animal in Aspen all that time. This is what he needed.

A face on a TV monitor attracted his attention. The face had a name, and it was – Hammond ... Vardis Hammond. The reporter in the picture Rico had in his pocket. Behind the man's face footage of a block war was playing; it looked like fun, the kind of fun Rico had always enjoyed the most.

Walking on Rico saw a large vid-sign hanging over a shop front, its message changing as he watched: GEIGER'S BAZAAR, it flashed – SURPLUS – PAWN – STORAGE – VOUCHERS CASHED!

'That's my man!' grinned Rico, his teeth suddenly white in the ultra-violet light of a nearby game booth.

35

The inside of the shop looked like a madman's attic; stuff was piled high on the floor, shelves groaned under the weight of dusty merchandise and yet more junk hung from the ceiling and any spare wall space. The back of the shop was screened off by a reinforced chain-link fence and behind a greasy counter sat a man puffing on a foul-smelling cigar butt.

'We're closed,' he said.

'You just opened again, Mr Geiger,' said Rico. 'I've come for my package, I'm Lazarus.'

'Whyn't you say!' muttered Geiger, standing up and shuffling over to a door in the fence. 'Gimme a second, willya . . .'

'Lovely place you got here,' said Rico, scanning the shop.

'It might look like rubbish to you,' said Geiger, coming back out front holding a large box. 'But lots of this stuff is real antique, very valuable,' he went on, locking the door behind him.

Rico walked over to the fence and looked through it at what appeared to be a rusting metal sculpture. 'I thought they destroyed all the Atomic/Bacterial/Chemical Warriors after the last wars,' he said, pointing to the ABC robot.

'You can still collect them – if they don't work,' explained Geiger, handing the box over to Rico. 'Here you go, ah . . . Lazarus.'

'Thanks,' said Rico, using his thumbprint to unlock the box.

Geiger moved sideways to see what his mysterious visitor had received. To his amazement he saw a

36

folded Judge's uniform and a Lawgiver in the package.

'Don't touch that!' he yelled, as Rico went to pick the gun up. 'Whoever sent you that was no friend of yours, pal!'

'Oh? Why?' enquired Rico.

'Fire it and you're a dead man,' said Geiger. 'Only a Judge . . .'

Rico picked the Lawgiver up and pulled the trigger. Nothing nasty happened to him at all, but Geiger hit the floor dead. 'How do you like that? I must be a Judge!' he laughed.

Bending down he took the bunch of keys out of Geiger's lifeless hands and went over to the door in the security fence. He unlocked it and walked to the robot ABC Warrior; he removed a panel from its head. A twisted mass of cabling fell out into the light and Rico, squinting at what he was doing, began to work on the electronic innards of this veteran of a war that had ended over half a century before.

Swiftly, and with intense concentration, Rico's fingers flew over the complex jungle of wires, circuitry and near-obsolete silicon chips. Eventually his hard work paid off: contacts sparked, lights glowed and the smell of burning dust filled the air – electric life was flowing through the metal veins of the ancient robot. Rico stood back.

'Status?' said a computer-generated whisper. 'Commander? . . . Mission?'

'Status – personal bodyguard,' said Rico, going over

and taking a cigar out of Geiger's coat pocket. 'Commander – Rico,' he went on, striking a match and lighting it. 'Mission – we're going to war!'

Vardis Hammond may have been the Big Meg's top investigative reporter, but he didn't live in the lap of luxury. His apartment was quite small, but it suited him and his wife. It was comfortable, it was secure, it was home.

Though well after midnight, Hammond was still at work on his computer. He had one heck of a story to tell the residents of Mega City 1 and stories, as any journalist could tell you, didn't write themselves.

'Finish it tomorrow, Vardis,' said his wife, coming to look over his shoulder at what he was writing.

'This won't wait, Lily,' said Vardis, fingers pecking at the keyboard like idiot birds.

'What does that say – a conspiracy in the Justice sysytem? Powerful right-wing elements in the Council?' read his wife. 'Where did you get this information, dear?'

'It's called researching a hunch,' said Vardis. 'I just confirmed some suspicions I had that the street Judges aren't acting like the worst kind of bullies without permission – somebody high up is directing them, I'm sure of it.'

'You can't go on air and say this!' Lily's hand went to her throat. She suddenly felt cold.

'Why not? It's the truth . . .'

'It would be insane,' said Lily angrily. 'You could get killed!'

'They don't kill reporters, Lily – at least, not yet . . .'
Vardis looked at his wife and smiled a thin smile.

'A story like this could bring the entire Council
down,' whispered Lily. 'The station won't let you
broadcast it . . . surely?'

'They won't be able to stop me,' said Vardis. 'I was
wrong to waste my time investigating Dredd – the
problem is with the entire system, not just one Judge
. . . I've got to tell the people.'

The soft chime of a bell sounded in the hallway.
Hammond frowned and looked at his watch. Followed
by his wife he went and opened the door.

'Oh no!' he groaned as the door swung open.

A Lawgiver barked twice in quick succession, and
Lily's scream never had a chance to leave her throat.

Finding a parking space was only half the problem on
the streets of Mega City 1. It was often so crowded
that the only way to unpark was to ram yourself a
space to get your car back on the road.

Car manufacturers had taken this situation into
account by giving all the latest models ener-sorb
bumpers. With ener-sorbs, front and rear, you could
crash your vehicle into a brick wall if you wanted to,
it wouldn't matter one bit.

Luke Souza, who just wanted to get home after a
long night of clubbing, didn't care that the cars he
was parked in between didn't have ener-sorbs. The
sound of crunching metal, as he tried to create himself some space, merely made him laugh.

'It's so darn crowded in this place!' he told his girl-friend, ramming his car into reverse and stamping on the accelerator.

'Don't you just love the sound of breaking glass?' she giggled.

'Not as much as I . . .' Souza paused, his wing mirror filling with the reflection of a dark uniform.

Judge Hershey motioned for him to lower his window. 'Step out of the car, please,' she said.

'You got a problem, officer?' pouted Souza.

'Step out of the car, sir,' repeated Hershey, opening the car door and grabbing Souza's arm. 'You too, miss.'

'Get your hand *off* me!' yelled Souza, pulling himself out of Hershey's iron grip. 'I got connections with the Council!'

'Unicard, please,' asked Hershey politely.

'I said I got connections!' Souza angrily thrust his card at the Judge and watched as she ran it through her scanner. 'Does that come up on your little machine?'

'No. But the fact that you have a suspended license and three counts of driving while under the influence does, Mr . . .' Hershey looked back at the screen: 'Mr Souza . . . so I'm citing you for reckless driving.'

'Listen up, sister,' Souza wagged a finger at Hershey. 'I suggest you go and bother some other guy, Judge Whoever – when I said I had powerful friends I wasn't kidding!'

'Do you have a problem, Hershey?'

Souza whirled round to find himself staring at a

badge with the word DREDD on it; he stepped back and looked up at a chin that could break bricks.

'No problems, Dredd.,' Hershey pointed at Souza. 'Just a loud-mouth with a suspended license and three DUIs, nothing I can't handle.'

'L-o-o-k,' said Souza, boredom dripping off his words. 'Just tell me what this is going to cost, OK? Name your price, guys . . .'

'Say that again and I'll hang your teeth round your tonsils,' spat Dredd. He looked over at Hershey. 'Call Control for an H-wagon.'

'If you're taking me in I want my car towed to a safe place,' demanded Souza.

'The Law allows towing for a first offence,' Dredd informed the glowering young man. 'This is your fourth . . . how do you plead?'

'Me?' Souza looked puzzled. 'Innocent, of course!'

'Somehow I knew you'd say that,' smiled Dredd. 'But the verdict is guilty, and for a fourth offence cars get moved by . . .' Dredd looked at his Lawgiver and said: 'grenade!'

Jaws hanging open, Souza and his girlfriend watched, helpless, as his beautiful new car exploded.

'You can't do that!' wailed Souza.

'You broke the Law, you have been judged.' Dredd put his gun away.

'We've got company,' said Hershey, pointing at a group of dark figures walking towards them through the smoke.

'Judge Hunters?' It was Dredd's turn to look puzzled. Judge Hunters were the most feared people

41

in the whole Justice Department, combat trained and without a shred of human kindness. The men coming towards him all had their Judge Hunter guns and the one in front was holding what looked like a holo-warrant.

'Judge Joseph Dredd?' the leader enquired, holding the warrant up so Dredd could see his own picture.

'Yes,' he said.

'You are under arrest.'

'There's been some kind of mistake.' Dredd reached out to take the warrant.

'Don't move, Dredd.' The lead Judge Hunter's gun pointed straight at Dredd's heart.

'What's the charge?' asked Hershey, moving closer to her colleague.

'Murder,' said the Judge Hunter.

For the first time in his life Dredd felt as if he'd crossed the line drawn between Judges and ordinary Citizens. He was now on the wrong side.

Chapter 6

The Hall of Justice was quiet. The only sound in the long corridors was the footsteps of the Judge Hunters as they escorted Chief Judge Fargo down into the holding cubes.

The Judge Hunters stopped outside a particular isocube and one of them unlocked the door, pulling it open to reveal a man with thermo-plas chains joining his hands and feet.

'Joseph . . .' said Fargo, walking slowly into the cell. 'Tell me it isn't true . . .'

'I'm innocent of the charge, sir.' Dredd stood up in the presence of the Chief Justice.

'The Council is said to have absolute proof, Joseph,' sighed Fargo. 'There's to be a full court hearing.'

'Do you believe *them*,' asked Dredd, 'or me?'

Seconds passed as the two men looked at each other, both afraid of what they might see. Their friendship was a long one, their trust complete, but a charge as serious as murder could not be dismissed so easily by either of them. Finally the Chief Justice spoke:

'I believe you, Joseph,' he said. 'I'm sorry I had to ask.'

'I don't understand how this could've happened ...' frowned Dredd.

'Neither do I, and I'll use everything in my power to find out,' said Fargo. 'Have you chosen someone to defend you?'

'Judge Hershey.'

'Hershey?' said the Chief Judge, surprised. 'Why a street Judge?'

'I can trust her.'

'I hope that's enough,' Fargo said grimly. 'But you can rest assured that you'll have my full support – I'll make sure the truth comes out in court.'

Dredd watched his old friend turn to leave. There was nothing else he could do now but wait, chained like a common perp in a cramped cube. Alone.

The Council Chamber was packed, the atmosphere electric. All eyes in the place were staring at a huge vid-screen which was filled with the terrified face of Vardis Hammond.

'Dredd ... no, please ...!' he was shouting.

A loud explosion rattled the speakers in the Chamber, followed by the hushed whispers of the assembled crowd of off-duty Judges, Cadets and journalists. They were watching the vid taken by the security camera outside the Hammonds' apartment.

'Stop the recording!' ordered Judge McGruder. The vid-screen went blank. 'Before we continue I wish to make a personal comment ...' She turned to look at Dredd, sitting next to Hershey. 'I have followed your career from its beginning, Judge Dredd – and in my opinion you are the best we have. Nevertheless, I must tell you that I will not allow my personal feelings to get in the way of my prosecuting you. I hope that's understood.'

'I expect nothing less, Judge McGruder.' Dredd stared straight at McGruder. 'It's the Law.'

'The Court agrees with both Judges,' said Chief Justice Fargo. 'Let the trial proceed.'

A hushed silence fell in the Chamber, everyone turning to look at McGruder.

'The vid you have just seen is, at first sight, evidence that the defendant is guilty as charged – let it be marked as People's Exhibit A.'

'Objection, Your Honour!' said Hershey, rising to her feet. 'The vid is inadmissable as evidence.'

'It is?' said Fargo. 'Explain why, if you will, Counsel.'

'Your Honour,' Hershey picked some paper off the desk in front of her, 'I have here a sworn statement from Cadet Olmeyer, currently a Junior at the Academy . . .'

Heads swung to look at Olmeyer, sitting with the rest of the Cadets in the crowded gallery. He was trying his best to look cool and failing miserably.

'According to his instructors,' continued Hershey, 'although young, Cadet Olmeyer is an expert in all types of video graphics – top of his class for five years running in Computer Progamming and Image Manipulation, with four Honours Certificates. He also helped create Central's vid analysis system – in other

45

words, what he doesn't know about digital pictures isn't worth knowing . . .'

'I think you've made your point, Counsel,' said Fargo, drumming his fingers. 'What does his statement say?'

'Apart from the fact that the Judge's badge could have been digitally altered,' continued Hershey, 'neither the pictures or the sound positively identify the accused in any way! I would ask you, Chief Justice, not to allow the vid to be used as evidence . . . Could we have a ruling, please?'

The other Judges on the bench looked at each other; Esposito and Silver appeared puzzled, while Griffin stared pointedly at Dredd. The crowds were mousequiet as they waited to hear what Fargo had to say, watching as his fingers drummed even harder on the desk.

'My ruling is . . .' he said finally, '. . . the video is *not* admissable as evidence.'

There was a roar from the crowd, although it was impossible to tell if they agreed or disagreed with Fargo's decision.

'Silence!' shouted Fargo, banging his gavel on the desk. 'This court is still in session – if I do not have immediate quiet I will be forced to clear the Chamber!'

This was a trial no one wanted to miss. Everyone shut up and Judge McGruder took a deep breath: 'I must accept the Chief Justice's ruling,' she said, 'but it will force me to ask the Court for permission to get Top Secret documents from the Central Computer.'

Hershey looked at Dredd; she hadn't been expecting this. She'd thought that by getting the vid removed as evidence there would have been no further case against him. What could McGruder be up to?

Judge Griffin leant across the desk and whispered something to Fargo, and the Chief Justice got nods of agreement from the rest of the Council. He looked back at McGruder. 'You have our permission,' he said.

McGruder, watched by everyone in the Chamber, crossed to a keyboard console and accessed the Central Command's computer. Her fingers flew over the keys and seconds later the Chamber's huge vid screen flickered into life and there, for all to see, was a massive cutaway diagram of a Lawgiver II.

Two parts of the diagram were outlined in red. The key at the side explained they were the areas of the Mark II that had been particularly improved over the earlier version of the gun.

'I will let Central describe the importance of the changes to the Mark II,' said McGruder, returning to her seat.

'Seven years ago,' said a cold, almost lifeless voice from the speakers, 'the Mark II Lawgiver was put into active service; it had two major refinements. The first was that, instead of just using the owner's palm print for recognition purposes, the Mark II is also coded to recognise the personal DNA of a Judge . . .'

'Did you know about this?' Hershey whispered to Dredd. He shook his head. 'Neither did I.'

'The second refinement,' said the voice from Central Command, 'was that each time a round is chambered

47

and fired, the Lawgiver II tags the projectile, or bullet, with the weapon owner's DNA code.'

'This is all very interesting, Your Honour,' Hershey stood and spoke to the Chief Justice, 'but could we be told what it has to do with the case against my client?'

Fargo looked at McGruder and raised an eyebrow.

'Your Honour, if Counsel would let Central finish . . .' said McGruder. Fargo waved a hand. 'Central, could you tell us if the bullets removed from Vardis and Lily Hammond were DNA coded?' she enquired.

'They were.'

'And whose coding was found to be on those bullets?' she asked.

'Judge Joseph Dredd's,' came the cold reply.

The uproar seemed to shake the Council Chamber to its very foundations. All around hands waved, fists punched the air and voices bellowed. It was pandemonium, and in the middle of it all Dredd stood and almost lost his temper.

'It's a lie!' he yelled above the noise. 'I've been set up!'

Chief Judge Fargo hammered the bench with his gavel and slowly order returned to the Chamber. Throughout the whole incident Hershey had remained in her seat, silent. She knew there was no defence against DNA evidence, and, biting her lip, she watched Judge McGruder rise and face the Council.

'Your Honour,' she said, 'the prosecution rests its case . . .'

Six feet of armoured justice looks around at a world gone mad.

The Judge Hunters arrive to arrest Judge Dredd.

The verdict is read out at Dredd's trial. 'Let the
Freedom he stole from others be stolen from him.'

The Angel Gang taunt Dredd and Fergie in the Cursed Earth court-house.

Dredd and Fergie escape from the Judge Hunters on the Lawmaster bike.

Judge Hershey persuades Olmeyer to help her analyse the viewee.

Olmeyer and Hershey reveal the mystery in the viewee.

The ABC robot stands in the shadows, guarding the entrance to the Janus laboratory.

'I am destroying the Law to create life,' said Rico insanely. 'Look around you – this is the future.'

'No you don't, you jumped-up sardine can,' cursed Fergie.

Lawman Joseph Dredd has been judged – a Hero!

Chapter 7

In the cold light of the next day Chief Justice Fargo
sat, slumped in his chair, in the empty Council
Chamber. Near him stood Judge Griffin. The two men
could have been at a funeral.

'How could I have been so wrong about Dredd?' said
Fargo, his head in his hands. 'Both of them homicidal
... only this time we can't cover anything up.'

'We destroyed the Janus Project nine years ago,
Fargo,' said Griffin. 'We got rid of Rico and all his
victims – and no one ... no one ... knows you were
involved.'

'But everyone knows how close I've been to Dredd.'
Fargo sat back, looking up at the ceiling. 'The media,
they'll dig until the truth comes out – one of their
own has been killed by one of ours. It's the excuse
they've been looking for to try and pull us down!'

'You thought Dredd was different, that's why you
spared him; but you're right, it may not look quite
like that if it comes out,' said Griffin. 'You could take
the Long Walk, Chief Justice ...'

'That's just another way of committing suicide.'

'True, but by retiring and going out into the Cursed
Earth you'll be able to do two things.' Griffin put a

hand on Fargo's shoulder. 'Save Dredd from the death sentence . . . and keep the Janus Project a secret – for ever.'

The Council of Judges were back in the Chamber and the galleries were once again packed to bursting point. The Judgment was about to be announced. The job fell to Judge Esposito, and he stood to do it.

'In the charge of murder in the first degree,' he said gravely, 'we find Joseph Dredd guilty . . .'

Even though it was expected, the crowds gasped. A legend had been destroyed in one simple sentence. Dredd remained still, as if carved in stone, waiting to hear what the Chief Justice would say.

'You are aware, Joseph Dredd,' Fargo spoke directly to him, as though the two of them were the only ones in the Chamber, 'that the Law allows only one punishment for a crime of this nature . . . and it is death.'

The two men, friends for so many years, stared at each other. And the seconds ticked by . . .

'However,' continued Fargo, 'it is our tradition that a retiring Senior Judge has one last command. This being so, I hereby step down . . .'

'No!' Dredd, shocked, tried to get up out of his seat. Hershey pulled him back down.

'And before I take my Long Walk into the Cursed Earth,' Fargo looked over at Judge Griffin, 'my last command is for the court to show mercy to Judge Dredd, in gratitude for his many years of loyal service . . .'

The Chief Justice got out of his chair and made way for Griffin to take his place. Once comfortably seated he said: 'We will honour your Command, Justice Fargo ... and the sentence shall be – life imprisonment at the Aspen Prison Facility. To be carried out immediately.'

Dredd watched his old friend leaving the Council Chamber, at the last moment turning to look at him. In his tired eyes Dredd saw nothing but sadness. He no longer believed him to be innocent. From across the room he saw the Judge Hunters coming to take him away, and next to him Hershey was jumping to her feet.

'This trial is a joke!' she yelled. 'I demand an appeal ...'

'There is no appeal in this court, Judge Hershey,' replied Griffin harshly. 'Our decision is final.'

'I didn't do it,' hissed Dredd as the Judge Hunters took him away, 'you have to believe me, Hershey!'

'I do,' said Hershey.

From the high bench in front of him Judge Griffin was reading from the great Book of the Law.

'Let the betrayer of the Law be taken from the Courts,' he said. 'Let the freedom he stole from others be stolen from him – and let his armour be removed ... forever.'

Twenty-four hours after Judge Griffin had suggested he take the Long Walk, the ex-Chief Justice was watching the sun rise at the gates to Mega City 1. This was the Final Ceremony.

51

Standing, dressed in a floor-length duster coat, Fargo had his uniform, Lawgiver and badge, ready to hand over. A young female Cadet read more words from the Book of the Law, tears in her eyes; once she had finished she gave the book to Fargo and took his uniform, badge and gun. Another Cadet then stepped forward and gave him a Judge Pump Gun.

A line of Cadets raised Lawgivers above their heads and Fargo walked under the arch of weapons, out of the City he had once virtually ruled. For ever.

As the door in the city wall closed behind Fargo, another slammed shut behind Dredd as he was chained to his seat in the Aspen shuttle. His sentence was Life, but he felt like it should have been called "Living Death". The Big Meg was in his blood and he was going to miss it like a drowning man misses air.

Dredd couldn't believe he would never see Mega City 1 ever again, but he had been Judged, and the Law, as he knew in the depths of his soul, had to be obeyed. Even when it was wrong.

Judge Griffin returned to his apartment, pleased to have rid himself of two thorns in his side. Opening his front door he saw the sun rise slowly above the walls of the city, its dull red light streaming through the picture window and casting deep shadows across the main room. A fire was burning in the grate and near it stood a dark, brooding figure.

Griffin stood for a moment, not knowing what to do. He wasn't expecting visitors. He reached up, flicked the light switch by his shoulder and hidden spotlights threw their pale light down on to an outdated war machine, of a type he'd last seen in a museum.

Rico appeared from behind the ABC Warrior, grinning. 'Chief Justice Griffin,' he said slyly. 'It has a very pleasant ring to it, don't you think?'

'We were supposed to meet somewhere safe!' he snarled.

'I like to do things my way,' said Rico, looking behind the Judge. 'And if you close that door, this place is as safe as any ... Hammond's dead, Fargo's out the way and Dredd, well he's taken my place in that pig-sty of a prison facility at Aspen. Everything's perfect!'

'Except that I could've used Dredd. He respected me ... trusted me absolutely.'

'He respected the Law, Griffin.' Rico sprawled in a chair. 'And if he ever finds out what you did he'll blow you away, given half a chance. No ... you trust me now, and let Dredd see what I had to put up with for so long – after all, we have so much in common it'd be a pity for him to miss out on such an important part of my life.'

Griffin stood looking from Rico to the ABC Warrior and back to Rico; both man and machine seemed to lack any respect for him, an experience he was completely unused to.

'As you're here, I suppose we'd better get down to work,' he said. 'There's a lot to be done ...'

'Janus!' Rico clapped his hands like a delighted child.

'Eventually,' said Griffin, 'but in the meantime I want chaos, Rico ... that block war at Heavenly Haven was just the beginning – I want fear to stalk the streets, I want panic! Then the Council will have to turn to me for help ... and I can unveil the Janus Project. Again ...'

'Chaos, fear and panic,' mused Rico, getting up to look out the wide apartment window at the stunning view it gave of the Big Meg. 'I think I can handle that, Chief Justice.'

Chapter 8

Dredd had paid little attention to the prisoner chained to the seat next to him. He didn't feel like talking to anyone, let alone a common perp. He could hardly believe what had happened; his life had been turned upside down in a moment of time and now he was on the outside looking in. Now he had guards treating *him* like a pile of dog mess, some piece of worthless garbage.

Among the many strange emotions he was feeling, confusion was probably at the front of the queue. Here he was, in a prison shuttle and on his way to Aspen. Every time he thought about it rage bubbled up inside him and made his muscles almost boil. He looked out of the window to calm himself down. It was then he noticed the way the man next to him was staring.

'Don't I know you?' said Herman 'Fergie' Ferguson, putting both hands up to his face and peering through the slit they made.

'I don't think so.' Dredd wanted to hit the man, but that would only cause him more trouble, and he had enough of that already.

'Judge Dredd!' whispered Fergie in amazement.

'Last time I saw you . . .'

Dredd looked at the man's face. He saw a picture of a shattered, blood-stained apartment block which seemed to belong in another life.

'Last time you saw me I gave you five years.' Dredd looked away.

'And now you're going to prison?' spluttered Fergie. 'What on earth for?'

'A crime I didn't commit.'

'Well, that makes two of us,' nodded Fergie.

'You got the sentence the Law required,' snarled Dredd.

'Five years for not wanting to be killed by a bunch of psycho nutcases!' Fergie's eyebrows hit his hairline. 'That's not fair!'

'The Law is always fair, it doesn't make mistakes.'

'Yeah?' said Fergie. 'Then how d'you explain what happened to you?'

'I can't.' Dredd yanked at his chains.

'So, if the Law doesn't make mistakes what was it?' enquired Fergie, half grinning. 'A bug in the system, maybe? A computer screw-up, perhaps? Or could it be, oooh . . . poetic justice?'

Dredd ignored his companion. He had to otherwise he'd have punched him. Punched him because, in a way, he was right. The Law had failed to see beyond the facts, failed to recognise his complete innocence.

But elsewhere on the shuttle Dredd had been recognised, not for what he was, but for what he had been – a Judge. Word travelled like a virus in a sick body, and soon whispered plans were being made to settle some old scores . . .

In the Cursed Earth there were the hunters and the hunted. And then there were the scavengers, half-human vultures and hyenas who lived off what the hunters left behind – unless the pickings had been bad, and then they'd make a kill of their own.

Of all the scavengers who inhabited the cruel outback the Angel family were the meanest, lowest, most vicious band of evil creeps ever to walk the desert sands. Heading the family was the Reverend 'Pa' Angel, his body covered in strange tattoos, and with him came his three sons: Link, Mean Machine and Junior.

All Pa's boys were violent, homicidal maniacs, but Mean had really earned his name; he had a mechanical arm and he'd been fitted with a dial on his forehead to control his nasty temper. 1, "mean", was as good as he got; 2 gave you "surly", 3 "vicious" and 4 ... well, 4 was the setting for "brutal". Which was not a pretty sight.

They were out looking for someone to eat when Junior spotted the Aspen Shuttle in the distance.

'Praise the Lord for what he has sent us!' nodded Pa. 'OK boys, we got us a harvest to bring in ... get the bazooka, Junior!'

'Gonna cut us down a crop of tasty city boys!' grinned Junior, unpacking an old-fashioned rocket-launcher and loading it with a magnetic time-bomb.

He heaved the weapon up on his shoulder and looked through the sights, carefully taking aim at the approaching shuttle. His finger hovered over the trigger and when he was sure there would be no mistake he pulled it.

A dull *WH-UUUMP*!! deafened the Angels, and they all watched, fascinated, as the rocket soared into the iron-blue sky. It twisted, snake-like, in the hot, dry air, zeroing in on the unsuspecting shuttle as it lumbered towards Aspen.

Dredd was street-wise enough to know that the atmosphere in the caged area where the prisoners sat had changed. There was a buzz in the air and, he thought to himself, you could have cut the tension, if you'd had a knife.

He almost didn't hear the sharp grunt behind him, and it was Fergie who saw the hand shoot from between their seats. It was holding a short, ugly blade.

'Dredd!' he gasped. 'Watch out!'

'It's payback time!' hissed the perp behind him, jabbing at Dredd's throat.

'The account's closed, dirtbag,' said Dredd, his reactions blindingly fast. His hand shot up and gripped the man's wrist, and he was about to crush the delicate bones when there was an awesomely loud explosion from the back of the shuttle and all the lights went out. The Angel's time-bomb had gone off.

Alarms shrilled, drowning out the cries of the manacled prisoners, and the air was filled with a ghastly roar as the hole blown in the shuttle's skin depressurised the cabin. The perp who'd been trying to stab Dredd suddenly shot backwards and was sucked out into space, screaming. Outside the cage one of the guards lost his balance and stumbled against the bars, his gun going off; bullets tore into the already bloody confusion, a stray one piercing the bulkhead and killing one of the pilots.

The shuttle dipped and yawed as the co-pilot fought to control it, but everyone on board knew he hadn't got a chance. The flying machine had turned into a falling machine, and there was no way to turn it back again.

'Hold on,' Dredd told Fergie. 'We're going to crash.'

'You don't say!' Fergie shook his head. 'Gee, I'm *so* stupid I didn't realise . . .'

'Hallelujah!' beamed Pa Angel, as he watched the shuttle go into a nose-dive, smoke pouring from its damaged belly. Beside him his boys whooped and hollered like kids at a rodeo. 'That was fine work, Junior.'

'Thanks, Pa,' he said.

'Don't thank me,' said Pa. 'Thank the Lord, boy.'

'Amen,' said Link, Mean and Junior, as the shuttle hit the ground and broke into three flaming pieces.

The Angels watched the centre section shoot sideways, the front of the shuttle continuing to plow forward until it hit some big rocks and stopped. Silence returned to the Cursed Earth, and then Pa spoke up: 'No point in standing round and looking, boys,' he said. 'We got us some work to do, and we don't want no other greedy hands trying to help us, now do we . . . ?'

*

59

The speed at which disaster had struck meant that the co-pilot of the stricken craft was only just beginning to send a Mayday signal when the shuttle hit the ground. Only half the message got through to Central Command, and it was early evening before the elite Capture Team of Judge Hunters found it.

Cold white beams of halogen light had stabbed the gathering dark, the lead Hunters sweeping the desert floor with powerful torches; finally the burnt-out shell came into view.

The team began moving through the wreckage, systematically scanning the bar codes on the tags of everyone they could find. It was grisly work, but the Hunters didn't care; a body was just a body, even if bits were missing. The details of each victim were logged and then immediately sent back to Central to be checked against the list of crew and prisoners.

Ducking through a gaping hole in the fuselage a Hunter called to his squad leader, beckoning. 'We've found tracks, sir,' he said. 'They lead away from the wreck . . . looks like at least seven people.'

'Capture Team to Central,' the Squad Leader spoke into his helmet mike. 'No sign of Dredd, he appears to have survived the crash. Repeat, he appears to have survived the crash. Instructions?'

'Your last message has been erased, Squad Leader.' Chief Justice Griffin's voice crackled in the Squad Leader's earpiece. 'You must have made a mistake. Dredd did not survive the crash . . . no one survived – do I make myself clear?'

'Yes, *sir*!' said the Squad Leader. 'Quite clear.'

A third Hunter joined the group standing by the hole in the side of the shuttle. 'We've found someone, sir,' he said excitedly. 'Alive!'

'Shoot him,' said the Squad Leader.

While the Judge Hunters poked through the remains of the wrecked Aspen shuttle, Hershey was silently slipping into the locker rooms in the Hall of Justice. She was allowed to be there, she was a Judge after all, but she didn't want anyone to know what she was doing.

Hiding in the shadows until she was sure no one else was there, Hershey darted over to Dredd's locker and took out a tungsteel jemmy. She was about to prise open the door when she heard a noise. Heart pounding, she peered round the corner. It was only a Cadet on cleaning duty . . . she relaxed and went back to work.

One swift shove of the jemmy, a soft KRAK! and the locker door was open.

Hershey began rummaging around on the shelves . . . towels, a second helmet, bits and pieces: brass polish . . . one, no two cans; boot polish, brushes, squares of cloth. Hershey was about to give up when, right at the back, pushed out of sight, she found a small leather slip-case.

'What have we here?' she muttered, shaking its contents into her hand. 'A viewie?' She frowned, moving into the light so she could see the picture. It was of a young couple and their baby.

'Well, well, well!' Hershey tapped the picture, nodding as she did so. 'So, Joseph, you were a baby – once!'

She was about to put it back when something made her turn it over and look at the back of the frame. What was that – a tab? She put her nail underneath it and pulled, revealing a second, hidden frame ... and a second viewie.

'So you did have a friend,' whispered Hershey. The picture showed Dredd – maybe 20, 21 years old – standing next to another young man of the same age. Both wore Cadets uniforms and were grinning broadly. 'Graduation Day,' said Hershey. 'I wonder who the other guy is?'

Footsteps echoed in the distance and Hershey could hear the voices of a group of Judges approaching the locker room. She closed the slip-case and put the viewies into her pocket, shut the locker door and slipped away.

Back in her apartment Hershey changed, showered and got a clean uniform ready for the next day. With a steaming cup of synthicaff in one hand, and a viewie in the other, she sat down at her computer station and asked it to connect her to Central's graphics database.

Putting the viewie of Dredd and his companion into a slot in the station she waited until it appeared on her screen and then put her finger on the man standing next to Dredd.

'I want an ID on this person,' she said.

'Scanning for identity,' said the Central Computer. Nothing happened for a long moment, then he went on: 'Unknown male, approximately two metres tall, 95 kilos, skin tone three . . . ten, nine, eight, seven, six . . .'

And then the screen went blank.

'Central?' said Hershey. 'Central . . . hello?'

A Judge emblem came up on the screen. *'This-terminal-has-been-disconnected-from-the-system-so-it-can-be-checked,'* said a digitised electronic voice. *'You-no-longer-have-access. Thank-you.'*

The viewie popped out of the slot. Hershey stared at the screen. This was just too weird.

Chapter 9

Chief Justice Griffin, Rico and the ancient ABC Warrior robot were making their way along a dingy, steel-clad corridor. Dim lamps set in the low ceiling cast pools of dirty light through which the trio passed in silence.

Griffin stopped by a door set in the wall and put his hand on its security pad. The door hissed open to reveal a large, circular room that obviously hadn't been used for years.

'Welcome to the Janus Project,' said Griffin, waving Rico through the door.

As Rico walked into the dusty room his eyes caught a movement in the shadows and he stopped to look at someone he hadn't seen since he'd been sent to Aspen.

'I think you two have met before,' said Griffin.

'Dr Ilsa Hayden,' Rico almost spat her name. 'You were kind enough to testify before the Council that I was insane ... and therefore innocent of all charges.'

'I was trying to help,' said Dr Hayden.

'You lied,' said Rico. 'I knew exactly what I was doing – then and now!'

'Really?' Hayden's eyes narrowed as she watched Rico pace the floor in front of her.

'Dr Hayden has kept the Janus Project alive for me, Rico,' said Griffin, eyes darting between the two of them. 'I'm sure both of you will get along . . . ah, wonderfully.'

'You do understand,' said Hayden, giving Rico a compu-pad, 'I can't get everything up and running without a complete re-fit.'

'Do me a . . .' Rico was about to rubbish Hayden's comment, and then he saw what was listed on the compu-pad's screen. 'Inducers, nitrogen coils, nano pumps! Heck, why not just nuke the place and start again?'

'There is a way,' said Griffin, 'a middle road . . . I think I can get everything we need from Mega City Hospital – they won't even notice it's missing. And if I'm right, when can you get Janus working?'

'Tomorrow!' Rico and Ilsa said at the same time. They stared at each other again, the tension between them obvious for all to see. Griffin couldn't work out if they hated each other, or were fascinated.

'But "on-line" won't mean drokk if we can't get into Central's Janus files,' said Rico. 'And, as far as I know, they're locked up so tight ain't no way we're gonna access them.'

'Leave that to me,' smiled Griffin. 'Remember, I am Chief Justice now. And in the meantime, you have work to do, out on the streets . . . Ilsa will help you.'

'I don't need anyone's help,' Rico told him.

'I thought you said he was state-of-the-art, Griffin,' sneered Ilsa. 'What did you call him? "A bold experiment in genetic engineering"? Some mistake, surely . . .'

'That's enough bickering, both of you,' scowled Griffin. 'We're all supposed to be working towards the same thing – a new society ... a clean, efficient, ordered world.'

'You'll get it, Griffin. All in good time,' said Rico, turning and whistling at the ABC Warrior waiting patiently at the door. 'C'mon, Fido ... time for walkies.'

Scattered everywhere across the Cursed Earth were memories of the way it used to be, before the wars had destroyed the world forever. Like decaying teeth the remains of buildings stuck out of the ground, ragged against the night sky, and gave shelter to the radiation-blasted scavengers who survived in that awful place.

Inside what had once been a Court House, back when being innocent until proved guilty was a right and Justice was fair, Dredd and Fergie were hanging by their cuffed wrists from the balcony of a filthy room. They were both unconscious.

Nearby, Pa and Link Angel were sorting through a pile of equipment the family had taken from the wrecked shuttle. As they busied themselves the quiet was shattered by a scream from outside the building. Mean and Junior were making someone's last minutes of life a complete and utter misery.

The scream brought Dredd and Fergie back into painful consciousness.

'I must've died and gone to Hell,' moaned Fergie.

'You should be so lucky,' grunted Dredd, seeing Pa Angel walk towards them.

'Awake . . . that's nice, we were just running out of sinners,' said the old man, as Junior and Mean came into the building, dragging the body of the shuttle guard they'd just killed.

'Good Grud . . .' said Fergie. 'Dredd, you gotta do something!'

'What did you say?' said Pa Angel, twisting Dredd round so moonlight fell on his shoulder, revealing the emblem all Judges had tattoed there. 'Oh, we are indeed blessed by the Lord!' He raised his arms and laughed. 'All we wanted from that evil machine was food and guns – but You have brought us the great man of Law hisself . . . Judge Dredd!'

'You're all under arrest!' growled Dredd.

'Is that so?' yelled Mean, rushing forward. Moonlight glinted on his forehead dial – it was set to No. 1. 'Let me crush his skull, Pa!'

'We're not together,' said Fergie, trying to turn away from Dredd. 'I've never seen him before in my whole life . . .'

'Allow me to introduce my family,' said Pa, ignoring Fergie. 'There's Link and Junior – my youngest boy.' They stepped into the light and grinned. 'And that's Mean, he had an accident as a child . . .'

Mean was staring at Dredd, dribbling.

'But I'm just being polite,' Pa went on. 'Cos you are acquainted with us, ain't you, Dredd? You remember killing my boy, Fink, don't you?'

'How could I forget the legendary Angels?' Dredd

looked at each one in turn. 'Cursed Earth pirates, scavengers and no-goods – didn't miss anything, did I?'

'I didn't hear that,' moaned Fergie. 'I wish I hadn't heard that . . .'

'True, all true,' smiled Pa. 'Mean, say "hello" to the nice Judge, why don't you?'

'My pleasure!' said Mean, flicking a jagged blade out of his mechanical arm and dragging it down Dredd's chest. The cloth split and blood spread across it.

'Sad, though,' mused Pa, scratching his chin and then reaching over to crank Mean up to No. 2. 'You still seem to be putting your faith in the false Law, instead of the One True Lord.'

'Let me kill him, Pa!' snickered Junior.

'I'm oldest,' butted in Link. 'I should go first!'

'Get outta here!' snarled Mean, tracing the shape of Dredd's tattoo with his dagger. 'He's mine . . .'

'Praise the Lord,' wailed Fergie in desperation. 'I have seen the light!'

Dredd looked over his shoulder at his companion, frowning.

'Can it be?' said Pa, amazement in his voice. 'Can someone from that doomed city be one of the Faithful?'

'Amen to that, brother Angel!' beamed Fergie.

'Why, you little creep . . .' Dredd could hardly believe what he was hearing.

'Boys, we have a True Believer among us!' Pa was almost in tears. 'Cut him down!'

'The gates of heaven are opening now!' added Fergie, as Link and Junior cut him down. 'I'm free and you're toast, Dredd,' he whispered. 'Tell that to the Law!'

'I might be toast,' Dredd whispered back. 'but you're the main course – I forgot to mention, the Angels are cannibals . . .'

'Fresh meat!' cackled Junior, helping Fergie to the ground.

'It's been fun, Lawman,' said Pa, turning Mean up to No. 3 and watching as his idiot son slammed his head into Dredd's face.

'Small, but tasty,' Link said, squeezing Fergie's arm. 'Just how I like 'em.'

'Prepare him!' ordered Pa.

'I'm not fresh!' screamed Fergie. 'I haven't washed in weeks – I've got bad breath, spots and ingrowing toenails . . . I wouldn't feed me to a dog!'

'Shut up,' said Pa. 'I hate food that talks back – and Mean, finish Dredd off.'

While the rest of his family began dragging Fergie off, Mean, with a crooked smile on his face, reached up and switched his dial to No. 4. Then he put his head down and ran full pelt at Dredd.

Because he was looking at the floor Mean didn't see Dredd swing himself sideways. With a wild bellow, the crazed Angel thundered straight into the wooden pillar supporting the balcony and split his head open. The impact shattered the pillar and Dredd fell to the floor, his hands coming loose.

He leapt on Mean, turning his dial down to No. 1,

and took off after Fergie and the other Angels. Pa, seeing him coming, ducked out of the way and scurried back towards his dazed son and yanked his dial back up to 4.

'Gonna get you now!' screamed Junior, drawing his gun.

Dredd's fist ploughed into his stomach and he grabbed Junior's gun and fired it at Link. Fergie was nowhere to be seen.

'Leave my boys alone!' howled Pa, picking a metal bar off the floor.

His arm was raised above his head, about to throw the bar at Dredd, when automatic weapons fire threw him off his feet. From nowhere Dredd saw the room fill with Judge Hunters.

'Out of the frying pan . . .' he muttered, leaping for the balcony and pulling himself up on to it. As he ran along the wooden floor, bullets punched fist-sized holes behind him and with a loud groan the whole thing began to collapse; '. . . and back into the fire again.'

Dredd dived straight at the Judge Hunter below him, knocking him senseless, then grabbed the one coming from behind. 'Hope you're bullet-proof,' he said, swinging him round to use as a shield.

The struggling Hunter's finger locked on his trigger, spraying the next man through the door with bullets; Dredd then grabbed the Hunter's gun and floored him with the butt. He scanned the room for more trouble, and what he saw was Fergie making a dash for a hole in the wall and running into two more Hunters.

'I surrender!' cried Fergie.

'Too late,' said one of them, about to fire.

'How true.' Dredd fired first, shooting at the legs of the two Hunters and then scrambling over the rubble to knock them out.

'Why didn't you kill them?' panted Fergie.

'They weren't shooting at me,' replied Dredd, slowly calming down from his battle frenzy.

'Yeah, well, I woulda helped,' shrugged Fergie, 'but it looked like I woulda just been in the way.'

A shadow, blacker that the velvet night, flitted across the doorway behind Dredd, and Fergie, eyes wide, pointed and yelped. Dredd whirled round to find himself staring at the business end of a Judge Hunter Gun. It looked like someone was about to type the words "The End" on the story of Judge Joseph Dredd.

Chapter 10

But it never happened. The air was split by the roar of a Judge Pump, and the Judge Hunter was dead before he hit the floor.

'Fargo?' Dredd looked over at the figure silhouetted in the court-room doorway. In his arms he was cradling a smoking pump-action, and Dredd could see moonlight glinting off his teeth as he smiled. 'How . . . ?'

But Fargo didn't have a chance to answer. From out of the gloom came a pain-crazed Mean Angel, his dial jammed past 4; he charged at Fargo and plunged the dagger on his mechanical arm into the ex-Chief Justice and lifted him up in the air.

For a moment Dredd couldn't do anything, frozen by the sight of the horrifying scene in front of him. Mean stood triumphant, with Fargo raised above him, laughing insanely at Dredd.

'Kebab time!' he yelled.

'You son-of-a . . .' Dredd blasted Mean with the gun he'd taken from the Hunter. The shot punched Mean backwards and he dropped Fargo; screaming in agony he stumbled out of the old Court House, roaring at the night.

Dredd and Fergie ran to Fargo's side. The front of his dusty overcoat was covered in blood and the stain was getting bigger. The life was flowing out of him, and there was nothing Dredd could do to stop it. The only link with his past was dying in front of his eyes.

While Dredd watched over his old friend in the Cursed Earth, back in Mega City 1 Judge Hershey was cursing Cadet Olmeyer.

'You want what?' she hissed.

Olmeyer sat back from his work station in one of the Academy's darkened classrooms. 'I want you to go with me to the Junior Dance,' he smiled sweetly at Hershey. 'I've given up on the idea of having you in the calendar ... I'll settle for a date.'

'I cannot believe the younger generation!' snarled Hershey, shaking her head. 'I'm busting my gut here to prove Dredd's innocence and all I get is you trying to *blackmail* me?'

'It's a tough old world, sir ... You got to take your chances where you find them.' Olmeyer bent back over his console. 'I've almost got the viewie processed – do we have a deal?'

Hershey nodded "Yes", but in a way that said she'd rather have head-butted the cocky young man sitting in front of her.

'Fine,' grinned Olmeyer, tapping a series of keys. 'We have a full Graphics Analysis coming up ...'

The screen cleared and then threw up the picture Hershey had found of Dredd and his parents.

'You *idiot*, Olmeyer – that's the wrong picture!'

'Sorry?'

'You were supposed to scan this one!' Hershey groped around on the desk and picked up the viewie of Dredd and his friend at Graduation Day. 'You've just wasted three precious hours of my time . . .'

'Hold on,' said Olmeyer, peering at the computer screen as a small window appeared at the bottom of it. 'There's something very wrong with this picture – it's a fake, Judge Hershey!'

'Say what?'

'It's not normal,' said Olmeyer, highlighting various areas of the picture and looking at what the computer told him about them. 'Somebody spent a lot of time on this, used a load of heavy-duty software too.'

'It's not real?'

'About as real as the Tooth Fairy,' muttered Olmeyer. 'Look, I'll get the machine to wipe out all the artificial pixels and we'll see what's left.'

Hershey's eyes were fixed on the shimmering screen, her mouth slightly open as she watched the picture in front of her slowly fade away.

'Sky . . . foreground . . . house . . . parents,' counted Olmeyer. 'All fake. In fact the only thing that hasn't been added to this happy little snap is the baby.'

Stunned, Hershey reached for a chair and sat down. She knew she'd just found out something incredibly important, but for the life of her she couldn't figure out what it meant.

'Get me a synthicaff,' she said.

Dredd had tried to make Fargo as comfortable as possible, clearing a space in the rubble and making a pillow out of some rags for his head. The old man looked terrible, his skin pale as milk, his cheeks drawn and sunken. You didn't need to be a doctor to know he hadn't got much time left.

'Water . . .' the old man croaked.

'Find him some,' Dredd told Fergie, who was hovering nervously in the background.

''Kay,' said Fergie, relieved to be able to get away. He hated the idea of watching somebody die.

'Good to see the blind lady again,' whispered Fargo, staring past Dredd at a statue high up on the wall next to him.

'Who is she?' asked Dredd.

'She represents Justice, the way people used to think of it,' explained Fargo quietly. 'Everyone was treated the same and justice was blind to everything but the facts . . . and once those facts were before the people, the jury, *they* decided the fate of the accused, not us . . . sometimes the old ways are the best, Joseph . . . sometimes I think we should never have taken control like we did.'

'It had to be done, sir.' Dredd knelt down by Fargo. 'And by doing it you brought order to chaos.'

'True . . .' Fargo lapsed into a blood-spattered coughing fit, reaching up to wipe his mouth before carrying on. 'We solved many problems, Joseph, but we also created many more . . . I can see that now, clear as dawn.' He coughed again. 'I'm dying, and know what? I'm glad I'm doing it here . . . closest thing to a church I know.'

75

'You're not dying.' Dredd looked away as he spoke, not wanting the lie to show on his face. 'I'll patch you up and take you back to the City . . .'

'Don't try and make it any easier . . . I know what's happening,' said Fargo. 'And now that it is, I've got to tell you something that happened before; I've got to tell you about the Janus Project.' Grabbing Dredd's hand, Fargo pulled him closer. 'I once tried to create the perfect Judge!'

'Forty years ago DNA samples were taken from every member of the Council,' he continued. 'The best was chosen – mine, as the Fates would have it – and the genetic engineers altered the sample to remove my weaknesses and boost my strengths . . . and from it we created . . . you . . .'

'But I had real parents,' frowned Dredd. 'They died when I was a baby . . . I've got a picture . . .'

'Lies,' said Fargo. 'There wasn't a word of truth in your files – we lied to both of you!'

'Both?' Dredd stiffened. 'Who else was involved?'

'We used the engineered sample to create two Judges,' Fargo looked away from Dredd, not wanting to see his face when the final chapter was told. 'But something went horribly wrong – you were everything we had hoped for, but for some reason he mutated into the very opposite.'

'I have a *brother*?'

'You were best friends at the Academy,' wheezed Fargo. 'Our star pupils . . . and then he turned and you had to judge him . . .'

'Rico . . .?' Dredd's mind was in turmoil; what had

been like a bad dream – watching the person he admired most in the world die slowly – was now turning into a waking nightmare. 'You let me judge my own brother and you didn't tell me?'

'I was, in almost every way, your father,' said Fargo. 'How do you think I felt? Rico was bad, evil, and part of him was me. He had to be killed to protect you – to protect the city.'

'You mean, protect the Council.' Dredd massaged his temples, trying to calm himself down. 'To cover up the fact you'd all helped create a monster.'

'Yes,' agreed Fargo, 'I can't deny that. The Janus Project was closed down, we couldn't allow him to live.'

An awful silence fell as Dredd tried to make sense of the lies and truths about his life, and then an incredible thought hit him and he felt light-headed, almost as if he was about to faint. 'He's not dead ... Rico's not dead!'

'I signed the order myself,' Fargo whispered. 'It happened.'

'No!' Dredd couldn't help raising his voice angrily. 'It was the DNA evidence that convicted me of Hammond's murder, and you just told me we shared an identical gene source – Rico and I have the same DNA, Fargo! He killed that reporter and his wife, not me ...'

'That can only mean ...' Fargo's eyes widened and his chest heaved with a racking cough, '... it was Griffin – it's got to be him behind this, Joseph. Go back and stop the two of them doing any more damage!'

A hollow sound, more of a rattle than a cough, came from Fargo's throat and Dredd grabbed the old man's hand. 'Don't die!' he said.

But Fargo wasn't listening any more. Dead men can't hear.

Chapter 11

When part of a body gets sick, very often the illness spreads – particularly if the body is weak in the first place. Mega City 1 was in a bad way, had been for years; too many people crammed into too little space and every system running close to breakdown. There had always been problems, but now they seemed to be getting out of hand. To those who knew the full picture, it looked like the sickness was running wild . . .

Downtown there was unrest in the financial district – a squad of Judges almost wiped out when a bank was bombed.

Six Judges, out sweeping a rat-infested warren of alleys and passageways, mown down by an unknown terrorist armed with a high-powered cannon.

Dozens of individual Judges picked off by a hidden sniper using armour-piercing bullets. Every single one dead before they hit the tarmac.

Block wars breaking out like a rash. For absolutely no reason.

And worst of all, in the heart of the Law itself, a micro-nuke took out an entire floor of the Hall of Justice. Carnage on a huge scale.

Temperatures were rising – but who could protect the Protectors if they couldn't look after themselves? Even with several shifts a day doubling up, the number of Judges being lost meant the Law was in danger of not being able to cut it any more.

What had very recently been five Lawmasters lay in a heap of tangled, smoking metal. The bodies of their riders, what was left of them, had been flung across the street by the frag-mines they'd accidentally ridden over.

Sunlight hardly ever reached this far down in the Big Meg. Any lower and you'd be in the sewers. In the early morning gloom a rat watched, head on one side, as a pile of rags shifted and moved and then got up. Two figures shook filth off themselves and walked away down the street, taking no notice at all of the horror they had just created.

'Like playing skittles,' said Rico, grinning wildly. 'BOOM! and they all fall down!'

'How much more d'you think they can take?' asked Ilsa.

'There's whole parts of the city out of control right now,' said Rico. 'Soon they're gonna be pleading for help – Griffin'll have the Council in the palm of his greasy little hand . . .'

It had been a hard journey, but then going anywhere in the Cursed Earth was never easy. After burying his old friend, with as much ceremony as was possible, Dredd had packed some provisions on to one of the Hunters' sand-cruisers, taken Fargo's Judge Pump and, with Fergie in tow, set off for Mega City.

Now they were standing about five miles from the walls of a place Dredd had thought he would never see again. Fergie wasn't so sure he wanted to see it, let alone get back inside. Although it was hotter than Hell itself in the Cursed Earth he was getting used to being a free man, even though he was travelling with a Judge. Or, more accurately, an ex-Judge and escaped prisoner.

Dredd was a strange man, thought Fergie. The system had trashed him, accused him of something he hadn't done (big surprise there), sent him to the worst prison in existence and then tracked him down like an animal. And he still believed in it!

Fergie had never believed in anything, certainly not the Law. Where he came from the Law was there for other people's benefit. But Dredd had another way of looking at it – to his weird way of thinking, the Law was neither good nor bad, it was just there. And if it was there it had to be obeyed. No questions.

He still acted like that out in the Cursed Earth. When you were with Dredd he was the Law, and you did what he said. Sometimes, thought Fergie, he even managed to make the Angel family look almost reasonable. Almost, but not quite – Dredd hadn't shown the least sign of wanting to eat him.

'There's no way in.' Fergie was watching Dredd scan the city walls through a pair of hi-gain, auto-powered digital binoculars. He ignored him. 'Ferguson to Dredd – come in Dredd! Did you get that? They ain't gonna put out no welcome mat, pal . . . no key to the front door under a flower pot!'

'I heard you.' Dredd lowered the binoculars. 'There is a way in; six years ago two Cursed Earthers figured it out.'

'How?'

Dredd turned back and looked across the heat-hazed scrub. 'There,' he said, pointing to a ball of flame that shot out of a hole low down in the city's wall.

'What the drokk's that?' said Fergie, just able to make out the smoke rising in a thin plume.

'That is a vent from the city's main incinerator, where the trash gets burned,' explained Dredd. 'There's a flame-out twice a minute, and that means there's thirty seconds for someone to get through the tube before the next fireball.'

'And those Cursed Earthers got back into the Big Meg that way?'

'No, they got fried.' Dredd packed the binoculars away and got a back-pack out of the sand-cruiser. 'But the theory's sound, so let's go . . .'

'Look, Dredd, it's hot enough to cook steak out here already,' whined Fergie. 'Why are we going to risk getting crisped in that exhaust pipe? I mean, there must be another way in . . . mustn't there?'

'Anyone ever tell you you sound like a tape loop – moan, moan, moan all the time?'

'It has been mentioned,' sighed Fergie.

'Well shut it and follow me.' Dredd slung the backpack on his shoulder and began walking.

Fergie shrugged and looked back at the Cursed Earth. It had come to something when that miserable expanse of desert and psycho-scavengers looked like the soft option.

Sirens in Mega City 1 had been like bird-song in the Old World, an everyday occurrence you hardly noticed. But now they wailed across the Big Meg continually, carried on the smoke-filled air, messages of disturbance and chaos that were all but drowned out by gunfire and screams.

This was a city in pain.

Lawmasters cruised the violent streets, their riders fighting fire with fire in the vain attempt to bring order back and bring the Citizens back in line. It wasn't working.

Deep in Green Quad, Judge Hershey was dealing with two looting perps in the only way she knew how. Slamming them against a chain-link fence, she cuffed them and yelled into her helmet mike: 'Dispatch! I got a 4–11 . . . I need a pickup!'

The response was agonisingly slow, the whole Justice system seemed close to collapse, but finally she got a reply. 'We copy, Hershey,' said an exhausted voice. 'We'll get one down there as soon as we can.'

'Right,' said Hershey. 'I'll leave 'em here . . . there's plenty more for me to do. Check with you later.'

'Wait up, Hershey,' said the voice. 'We got Central on the line for you; can you take it?'

'Patch them through to the Lawmaster.'

Followed by the yells and curses of the two cuffed looters, Hershey walked back to her bike. For a moment she thought her helmet speakers were acting up, but then she realised the droning noise she could hear was coming from elsewhere; looking around she saw all the street lights suddenly flicker, fade and then go bright again. She frowned, shaking her head as she swung her leg over the saddle.

It was then that she noticed a flashing red light on the Lawmaster's on-board computer display panel. It was pinpointing the underside of the fuel tank. Hershey bent down to look and saw something dark, something that shouldn't be there. And then the object emitted a high-pitched beep.

'Mag-bomb!' said Hershey, flinging herself off the machine and going into a rolling dive.

Behind her there was a sharp KRAKK! followed by a loud WHOMP!! as several hundred thousand creds of leading-edge technology disintegrated in a ball of flame. Curled up tight, Hershey waited until the hard metallic rain that had once been her personal transport stopped falling, and then she got up.

'Could've been me,' she said under her breath. And then she looked round at the two looters. Their bodies hung limply from the fence, where they'd taken the full force of the blast, unable to escape it. 'Dispatch,' sighed Hershey. 'We won't be needing that pickup any more . . . send some body bags instead. Over.'

Chapter 12

If the Cursed Earth had been a hot place it had got *nothing* on squatting under a garbage vent as fireball after fireball blew out like some kind of crazed giant of a circus act. Every thirty seconds night turned into day for a blistering moment and then darkness returned.

Fergie couldn't see properly, he had spots in front of his eyes so big they blotted everything out. Strangest thing was, they were still there in the dark. To add to his problems his head ached and his feet hurt and the last thing he was going to get from Dredd was anything remotely like sympathy.

FFFF—BOOOOM!

Another fireball burst the night apart and then died.

'Ready?' asked Dredd. It was the first thing he'd said to Fergie for at least an hour, but, in Fergie's experience, Judges were never much on conversation.

'No,' said Fergie.

'Something wrong?'

'Something *wrong*! Are you kidding?' exclaimed Fergie. 'I think wearing a tight-fitting helmet all these years has stunted your brain, Dredd. Of course

85

something's wrong – you're gonna get me killed, I have less than a minute to live!'

'We're wasting time,' growled Dredd. 'There's a maniac loose in the city, and I've got to get in there!'

'Don't give me "in the city",' snorted Fergie. 'There's one on the loose right here, and you're it! This is all your fault.'

'My fault?' Dredd found it hard to take a perp talking to him in this way. It had never happened before.

'Sure, If you hadn't arrested me on that stupid damaging-property charge I wouldn't be here now, up to my backside in Dante's drokking Inferno!' Fergie sat down and stuck his bottom lip out. 'I ain't going *no*where until you apologise.'

'The Law *never* apologises.'

'Well you *ain't* the Law no more, *Mr* Dredd,' said Fergie. 'So, apologise.'

The roar of an approaching fireball echoed down the vent above them.

'C'mon, no one's listening,' wheedled Fergie. 'Break the habit of a lifetime, you'll feel better for it – and what's more, you owe me!'

'I'li . . .' Dredd hesitated. 'I'll review your case . . .'

'Review is good,' nodded Fergie. 'Said almost like a human being, but . . .'

The next fireball roared into its short, violent life, drowning out what Fergie was saying. As it burst into the open air and flared itself to nothing, Dredd turned and leapt up into the vent.

'No time for "buts"!' he yelled, reaching down and dragging Fergie up after him. 'Let's get going!'

A clock began ticking in Fergie's head as he ran after Dredd: '... 29 ... 28 ... 27 ... 26 ... 25 ...' he counted out loud, suddenly aware he wasn't keeping up.

'Stop the damn counting!' Dredd shouted back.

'19 ... 18 ... 17 ... 16 ...' Fergie couldn't help himself, and he was also too exhausted to run any faster.

Not far in front of him Dredd could see a faint light – the air intake on the other side of the wall. He was yards from home! He looked round, expecting to find Fergie right behind him, but he was still only halfway up the massive pipe. Dredd could just make out his voice – '12 ... 11 ... 10 ...' and then he saw him trip and fall.

'Dredd! For Grudsake help me!' he shouted, tugging at his shirt. 'I'm caught!'

Dredd heard a sudden hissing from behind him, and the unmistakeable smell of high-octane kerosene gas filled the air. They were seconds away from ignition. He ran back towards the struggling figure on the ground as the electric contacts sparked and the gas lit.

'Don't let me fry!' wailed Fergie, eyes popping as he saw the fireball grow to full size up ahead. And then he noticed the gun pointing down at him. 'OK, so put me out of my misery like some kind of dog...'

Dredd fired the Judge Pump, blasting away the grate by Fergie's ruined shoes. It fell away, leaving a gaping hole, and Fergie knew what he had to do. With one last muscle-ripping pull he tore his shirt free and jumped into the duct below the vent. Dredd leapt after him.

A thundering roar rolled over him as he fell down the duct, superheated air burning his skin. He knew Dredd was tumbling after him, but he had no idea where they were going to end up. It could hardly be worse, he thought, thankful to still be alive.

In front of him he saw a pale grey shape getting bigger and bigger, and then he realised he was flying out of the duct. For a second it seemed like he was floating, then he landed in something warm and soft. A cloud of very fine dust filled the air and Fergie started to choke.

A second dull thud sent even more dust into the air. 'Where – kof! – are – kof! – we?' he spluttered.

'The ash pit,' wheezed Dredd.

Fergie sneezed. 'How do we get out of here?'

'There's an entrance, there must be an exit.' Dredd got up; he was covered in a thin grey film of dust and looked like something risen from the dead.

'Having a conversation with this man,' thought Fergie, 'is like talking to a telegram.'

In the Council Chamber lights burned far into the night. Minute by minute more bad news poured in and the Council Judges felt as if they were fighting a losing battle against an overwhelming tide of disaster. The situation was desperate and had all the signs of getting a lot worse.

'Latest casualty reports show 96 Judges assassinated,' said Judge Esposito, stabbing a finger at the piece of paper in front of him.

'Whoever's doing this knows all our procedures,'

McGruder said angrily. 'They've got inside knowledge of our security procedures – even our scrambled radio frequencies!'

The rest of the Judges in the room shook their heads in disbelief at what they were hearing. It couldn't be happening, but it was.

'With not enough Judges on the streets, riots are breaking out all over Mega City,' continued Esposito. 'In my opinion we've gone beyond breaking point.'

'I've looked at the figures,' sighed Judge Silver, 'and even if we put Cadets out there we'll be well below strength.'

This was the time Griffin had been waiting for. All his schemes and plans had been working towards this moment – the moment when everyone had lost hope and only he had the answer. He just managed to stop himself from smiling as he sat forward in his chair and cleared his throat.

'There is a solution,' he said. Everybody in the Chamber looked at him. He had their full attention, exactly the way he wanted it. 'The Janus Project,' he said.

'Chief Justice Griffin!' McGruder exploded, standing bolt upright and almost tipping her chair over as she did so. 'Just mentioning that disgraced programme is grounds for a criminal charge!'

The Chamber was in uproar, the whole Council outraged by Griffin's suggestion that they once again play the dangerous game of trying to create life. It had been tried before, and they all knew the outcome and they didn't want to be reminded of the awful, dark secret that they had had to destroy.

'If this wholesale slaughter of Judges continues, there'll come a time when there won't *be* a Council!' said Griffin. 'Janus could—'

'Janus could do *what*?' interrupted Esposito. 'Cooking up a laboratory full of test-tube babies won't solve this crisis — we don't need new Judges twenty years from now, we need them today!'

Griffin had anticipated this argument and he snapped back with the answer: 'Accelerated Growth Incubators, Esposito,' he said calmly.

'What?'

'We can now create adults, fully grown and fully trained at the birth-point,' said Griffin. 'We could replace all the Judges we've lost in a week. We have the technology, we have the knowledge — and much more important, we have the need!'

'I can't believe what I'm hearing,' said a stunned McGruder, sitting down again.

'All I'm asking is that we unlock the Janus files.' Griffin put his hands out, palms up, appealing for the Council's help. 'That way, my friends, at least we have an *option*.' He paused to let his words sink in. 'At least agree to look, if you then decide not to go ahead, I'll accept your democratic decision . . . and resign.'

The rest of the Council were silent, unable to speak. Griffin knew he'd successfully thrown the ball back in their court and if they went against him they would take the blame for the fast-approaching disaster. And if they went with him, ultimate power would be his, and his alone . . .

Chapter 13

While the Council were wrestling with the ghastly moral problem of what to do about Griffin's proposal, Tech clean-up crews were battling against the clock to repair the bomb-damaged Hall.

Debris was littered everywhere and emergency lighting, strung haphazardly from the blackened ceilings, cast deep shadows. And these made perfect hiding places.

Having got his update from a crew leader, a Judge made his way through the rubble. He was lost in thought, the news from the Techs was bad; with so many things going wrong all over the city, there just wasn't enough manpower to get the jobs done fast enough.

The Judge was jolted back to reality by a noise. It came from behind a pile of badly damaged lockers. The Judge stopped, puzzled; as far as he knew no one was supposed to be there, all the crews were working in other sectors. He hesitated, and then went to investigate.

Walking round the twisted pile of metal he stopped dead in his tracks. In front of him stood a grey figure dressed in what looked like ragged prison clothes.

And he was waving.

Fergie watched the Judge. The man obviously didn't know what to do, what he was seeing didn't make sense, and his confusion was his downfall. Before he had time to unholster his gun, or call for help, Dredd came up behind him and whacked him with a thick piece of metal pipe.

'If they catch me now,' muttered Fergie, watching Dredd strip the limp figure of its uniform, 'they'll give me ten life sentences and then put me up against a wall and shoot me . . . if I'm lucky.'

The Council had come to a decision. They too had worked out the bind they were in, realising that the Chief Justice had left them no choice but to agree to his demand. One by one each Judge fed his personal code into the central computer, the screen showing the data locks being removed from the Janus file.

Then Judge Silver walked up to the console. 'Silver, Gerald,' he said gravely. 'Council Judge. Authorize access to file, code name Janus.'

The job was done.

'I have unanimous authorisation to open the file, code name Janus,' said Central. 'I am removing security blocks . . . now.' The final data lock disappeared. 'I am awaiting the password command from the Chief Justice.'

This was the moment he'd been waiting for, and Griffin could almost smell the sweet aroma of success. 'Password . . . Origin,' he said.

'Janus file open,' replied Central.

Griffin stood up and moved over to the console. 'Central,' he said, 'how long, using current technology, would it take for Janus to create a fully grown adult?'

'Given the advanced level of genetic engineering that we have now reached,' replied Central, 'Janus could create and birth a fully programmed adult in approximately eight hours.'

'Eight hours?' McGruder couldn't hide her astonishment. 'But that's incredible!'

Now Griffin allowed himself to smile. He had the Council eating out of his hand.

Elsewhere in the Hall of Justice a Judge hauled a miserable perp down a corridor by the scruff of his dirty grey neck.

'Couldn't you be a bit more like *gentle*, Dredd?' said Fergie.

'No,' came the abrupt reply.

'Well can't I at least walk in front, you know, under my own steam?'

'Stop talking, you'll give the game away.'

'Doesn't feel like a game,' mumbled Fergie.

Dredd hauled him round a corner and Fergie saw another Judge approaching them. He was still some distance away, but he felt Dredd's hand tighten on his neck. Fergie had no idea where they were going, but he had a nasty feeling in the pit of his stomach that he didn't want to be there.

The other Judge, who seemed to be in quite a hurry, was reading some papers as he walked and hardly glanced at them as he passed. Fergie felt Dredd's fingers relax a little, and then they gripped even harder as he heard the Judge stop and turn to watch them.

'Recognise him?' whispered Fergie.

'Of course I do,' muttered Dredd. 'The point is, has he recognised me . . .'

The atmosphere in the Council Chamber was tense. The assembled Judges sat, almost pinned to their seats, as Central answered Griffin's questions about what Janus could do and how long it would take to do it.

The figures were truly incredible: a fully equipped laboratory, working at peak capacity, could deliver four programmed adults an hour – seven *hundred* a week, every week. It didn't take a mathematical genius to work out that, once up and running, Janus could replace all the Judges lost so far in just one day of operation.

No one could argue with the facts about Janus, but they could, and did, argue with the rights and wrongs of doing it again. To many round the table the project had already proved itself to be at best unworkable . . . and at worst a terrifying reality.

'It's utter madness!' shouted Esposito angrily. 'It is not for this Council to set itself up to play at being God!'

'We have the power,' Griffin said calmly. 'We must use it.'

'No!' McGruder slammed her hand down on the table. 'Judge Griffin, I am going to ask you to put back the data locks – any other course of action would be insane!'

Griffin could feel the Council slipping away, his hold on them loosening. 'It seems none of you have the guts that these desperate times require,' he snarled. 'Central – leave the Janus files unlocked!'

'This is treason!' McGruder pointed an accusing finger at the Chief Justice. 'You must be stopped!'

'You got that wrong, lady,' said a stranger's voice that came from behind Griffin. 'You're the guys that are gonna be stopped.'

A dark figure stepped into the room, a Lawgiver held loosely at his waist, its barrel pointing at the ground.

'Do it,' said Griffin.

'Rico?' McGruder sounded puzzled, as if she thought she must be dreaming, but her hand still went for the Lawgiver at her side . . .

Outside the Council Chamber Dredd could hear raised voices. He put his hand on the door and tried to open it but it was locked shut.

'Get back,' he told Fergie, raising Fargo's Judge Pump and pointing it at the lock.

'But, Dredd . . .'

'Do as I say, or you'll get hurt.' Dredd felt a hand on his shoulder and reached up to brush it off. 'I said—'

'I thought it was you,' said the Judge who'd passed them in the corridor. 'They let you back already?'

'I got a day pass for good behaviour.' Dredd swung round and slammed the butt of the Judge Pump into the Judge's head. 'Sorry, pal,' he said as the man crumpled to the floor, 'wrong time, wrong place.'

From the other side of the Chamber door came the angry crack of a Lawgiver, and the thud of slugs hitting the walls.

'What the . . .?' Dredd whirled round and blasted the lock two, three, four times. He heaved a boot up, slammed it against the door and ran into the room.

'You murdering son of a—' he began shouting at Griffin, who was standing, looking at a man holding a Lawgiver. And then Dredd saw Rico.

He was smiling down at his handiwork, grinning like a devil at the slumped, bleeding bodies of the dead Council Judges. In the distance alarm bells and raised voices could be heard, heavily booted feet thundered down long marble corridors.

'Get out of here now, Rico,' ordered Griffin, taking out his hand gun. Rico faded, ghostlike into the shadows without a word, still smiling.

'You're under arrest, Griffin.' Dredd turned the Judge Pump on him.

'Really?' said the Chief Justice.

Dredd's eyes were fixed on Griffin's face and he didn't catch the movement of the man's hand as he raised his gun and shot himself in the arm. For a second Dredd thought he was being fired at, and then he saw what the newly-arrived Judge Hunters saw as they burst in: the Chamber full of dead Judges, the wounded Chief Justice clutching at his blood-spattered arm and an escaped criminal holding a Judge Pump.

'Stop him!' yelled Griffin. 'He's just murdered the entire Council!'

Dredd had no alternative but to run. It went against everything he believed in, but all that mattered now was his own survival. He had to survive to get Rico and Griffin and make them pay for what they had done, to make them pay for trying to destroy the Law.

Dodging behind pillars he flew back out in to the corridor, making the most of the head start he got because the Judge Hunters had stopped to see if Griffin needed any help.

Jumping over the body of the Judge he'd knocked out, Dredd began running down the corridor.

'Wait for me!' yelled Fergie, appearing from behind the column where he'd hidden the moment things started to happen. 'I'm one dead hacker if they find me here!'

'Move it then!' grunted Dredd, ducking a salvo of bullets that ripped into the wall just ahead of him.

Zigzagging along the corridor, Dredd turned a corner and saw a door marked "Academy Training Centre"; he grabbed Fergie and dragged him into the unlit room. He knew they only had a few seconds before the Judge Hunters, dozens of them, would be pouring into the place. He had to find a way out, and fast.

Taking precious moments to work out where he was, Dredd's eyes found what he was looking for. Standing only a few yards away was the prototype Mark IV Lawmaster he'd had the techs demonstrate for the student class he'd taken just a few days before.

'If this doesn't work,' he said, running over to it and getting on, 'I've had it.'

'Make that "we",' said Fergie. '*We've* had it, plural – my ass is on the line here too, remember. Those guys don't care who they hit!'

As if to prove his point, the Training Centre door was flung open and a pair of Judge Hunters dived in, guns blazing.

'C'mon baby,' Dredd almost cooed, 'you can do it . . .' The bike's computer screen glowed, the engine fired and its wheels lifted off the ground. And then the engine began to cough.

'What's the matter with it?' yelled Fergie, by now sitting up behind Dredd.

'It's temperamental,' replied Dredd, punching the control pad and activating the machine's cannons. 'But I think we're going to make it.'

He jabbed the firing button and the twin cannons roared as the bike moved forward agonisingly slowly. The wall in front of them disintegrated; Fergie peered over Dredd's shoulder and through the smoke he saw a huge hole in it.

'That's M-M-Mega City out there,' he stammered.

'Sure is.' Dredd accelerated the machine, but the lifter motors still hadn't fired.

'But we're a *mile* up, Dredd!'

'Best place to be to see if this baby can fly,'

'Fly!' screamed Fergie. 'You out of your mind, Dredd?'

'No.' Dredd revved the engine until it was screaming, and then let out the clutch. The bike leapt forward. 'I'm out of this place . . . I hope.'

Chapter 14

Dredd was never a man with much time for prayer. Prayer was for those who couldn't make it happen for themselves. But now he was ready to ask anyone or anything that was listening for help. 'Please work, please work, please work,' he muttered, while behind him Fergie clung to him, sobbing.

A madness of exploding lead and tracer fire hit the brickwork around them as the bike sailed out into the wide night sky, shards of masonry digging into them like angry wasp bites. The Mark IV fell, as only a ton of metal could, dropping silently through the air.

'Pleeeeeeeeeease!' yelled Dredd, his eyes fixed on the bike's computer screen, waiting to see it tell him he wasn't going to end up spread across a couple of hundred square yards of tarmac.

As they plummeted towards the street the words "AERIAL MODE" flashed on the screen, followed a second later by the message "ON LINE". With a heart-stopping jolt the lifter motors roared into life and the bike stopped falling and blasted upwards.

'We're gonna die!' screamed Fergie.

'Not just yet!' Dredd yelled back.

Powering the Mark IV away from the Hall of Justice Dredd caught sight of a handful of Judge Hunters standing, helpless, at the edge of the jagged hole in the Training Centre wall.

'Where's the drokking seat belt, Dredd,' said Fergie, poking at his shoulder. 'I'm gonna fall off this thing!'

'If you don't shut up, we'll *both* fall off,' growled Dredd. 'I'm trying to figure out how to work this machine . . .'

'No point in asking about the air bag, then.' Fergie gripped Dredd even tighter and took the risk of glancing round to see where they were. He wished he hadn't. From behind the Hall of Justice he saw three more Mark IVs arcing out into the night sky in close formation. 'Oh Grud!' he moaned. 'Willya look at that!'

'I saw.'

'What're we gonna do?'

'You are going to cover our tail.' Dredd unslung the Judge Pump and handed it to Fergie.

'Me?' said Fergie. 'But I've never fired a gun in my life!'

'What kind of criminal are you?' asked Dredd, throwing the bike out of the way of some oncoming traffic.

'The peaceful kind that should never get sent to prison,' replied Fergie.

'Stop yakking and shoot the drokking gun, will you!' Dredd hauled the bike up over a low building.

Fergie pulled the trigger, but nothing happened.

'You have to take off the safety, you moron!' shouted Dredd.

'Now he tells me,' said Fergie, struggling with the

lever. It clicked. He took aim at the leading Hunter again and pulled the trigger. The shot hit the bike furthest away, and smoke poured out of one of its lifter ports. 'Yes!'

'Don't get too excited,' said Dredd, aiming the bike straight at huge 3D holographic vid poster, its multiple images flicking on and off, hard-soft-hard-soft. 'He's still flying.'

'Killjoy,' grinned Fergie, looking round. The smile fell from his face when he saw where they were heading. 'You can't go through that – the lasers'll slice us like bacon!'

'Only if we try and go through when the hard image is up.' Dredd powered the bike forward as the vid image flashed off and they were through to the other side of the holo-poster.

A different image flashed on as they zoomed away. Fergie looked back over his shoulder to see a Hunter zip his bike safely through the vid poster as it flashed off, while another shot through the narrow gap underneath it. 'Drokk! We got company still!' he said.

Then the third Hunter, the one on the damaged bike, tried to go the quick route through the holo-poster ... but he wasn't quick enough. While his machine was only half way out the other side the lasers snapped a new hard image up and he was caught.

There was a huge, blistering explosion as the hard light fried the rider and his Mark IV, a wave of hot, debris-filled air tossing Dredd, Fergie and their two pursuers around like waste paper in a storm.

'We've been hit!' Dredd yelled above the racket, a

102

cloud of smoke pouring from the bike. 'I'm going to have to take us down to street level.'

Fergie looked down. 'You can't do that,' he shouted back. 'It's bad enough up here, but there's a riot going on down there!'

Below them the streets were a surging mass of stampeding humanity; Rico and Ilsa's Judge slaughter had opened the flood gates and let the Citizens out of their cages, and there was no one left to put them back in.

'Whyn't you just drop me off, Dredd?' suggested Fergie, as Dredd brought the bike down on to the street, scattering the tightly-packed crowds. Behind them the two remaining Hunters began firing their cannons. 'Or maybe not . . .'

Up ahead Fergie could see they were speeding into a dead end – a real dead end, with a solid brick wall closing it off. If they hit that they'd be jelly. Fergie's life began flashing in front of his eyes – his boyhood dreams of being the ultimate software programmer . . . the pain and joy of growing up . . . his first girl-friend . . . the buzz of hacking into forbidden computer zones . . . all this and more was there as the bricks roared towards him until he could almost see each grain of sand in the cement holding them together.

And then Dredd did the impossible. He hauled the crippled bike up in a near-vertical climb and they were flying over the roof of the building they'd almost, but not quite, hit.

The leading Judge Hunter wasn't so lucky; he'd assumed Dredd wouldn't make it, and when he suddenly disappeared the Hunter couldn't help but look for him. His eyes flicked up, and in that split second he plowed into the wall himself, what was left of him and his bike redecorating the apartment they'd crashed into.

The Hunter following him was able to to take evasive action and power over the apartment building after Dredd and Fergie, cannons still blazing. Dredd's bike took another hit and slowed down even more, allowing the last Hunter to catch him up.

'You steer!' Dredd told Fergie, as the Hunter came level.

'Me?' said Fergie, horrified. 'I can't even steer a supermarket trolley!'

'Learn,' scowled Dredd, leaping off the bike and leaving Fergie staring at the empty seat in front of him and a vacant set of controls.

Dredd sailed through the air and landed on the back cf the Hunter's Lawmaster. The man hadn't even got time to be surprised by this unexpected turn of events before Dredd slugged him and threw him out of the saddle. His screams faded to nothing as he plunged earthwards.

Grabbing the handlebars, Dredd got the bike under control and chased after Fergie, who had closed his eyes and was heading straight for the top of an office block astride the terminally damaged Mark IV.

Swooping as close as he dared, Dredd plucked Fergie off the bike and powered up and away from the building. Fergie opened his eyes just in time to see the bike he'd so recently been in charge of slam into the office building and erupt in a ball of orange flame.

'I am *never*, not *ever* going to drive *any*where with you again! Hear me, Dredd?' screamed Fergie, so angry he could spit. 'If I get caught they're going to do things to me I don't even want to think about!'

'Calm down, Ferguson.' Dredd found himself almost smiling at the fact that he'd managed to get away. 'You're still breathing, be thankful for small mercies.'

Above the city, from an apartment so high up that the lights looked like a carpet of diamonds thrown on a piece of black velvet, Chief Justice Griffin looked down at where he knew the streets ran with blood and the air was filled with screams.

He would have laughed with satisfaction, but his arm still hurt from where he'd shot himself. Beneath the medivinyl bandage the wound throbbed dully, a constant reminder of how close he'd come to having his carefully-laid plans ruined by the surprise appearance of Dredd.

'Why didn't you kill him when you had the chance?' said a voice from behind him, and Griffin turned to see Rico walk into the room.

'Because I think things through, Rico,' said Griffin. 'He's more use to us still alive ... out there,' he pointed down at the city, 'taking the heat off us while we get Janus up and running.'

He walked over to his console and punched in his personal code. 'Central,' he said, 'prepare the Janus lab for full operation – and while you're on-line I'd like you to take note that I've appointed Judge Rico to the Council.'

'That may give us a few legal difficulties,' replied Central. 'Rico . . . my apologies, Judge Rico, is listed as having been executed nine years ago.'

'Your records are obviously not accurate,' said Griffin.

'We do not make errors,' said Central. 'Judge Rico must have been executed, if that is what the records say.'

'Change 'em,' grinned Rico. 'I just got all better again!'

Chapter 15

Hiding the Lawmaster behind some air-con units on the roof, Dredd and Fergie made their way down to Hershey's apartment. It was an easy job because all the security was at the entrance, no one was expected to come in from above.

As they walked along the corridor to the unit where she lived, Dredd suddenly stopped and unslung the Judge Pump. Even from where he stood he could see Hershey's door had been forced open and was hanging from its hinges.

Pushing it wide using the gun's barrel, Dredd slid into the darkened room and switched a light on. The place had been frag bombed; wrecked furniture was everywhere, the computer console smashed and pictures torn off the walls.

'Either she had quite a party, or someone's been here before us,' said Fergie, watching Dredd creep silently over to the bedroom door. 'Whatever, I think we should get outta here before anyone else turns up.'

Dredd ignored him, opened the door and went in. Too late, he sensed he wasn't alone and the next thing he knew a gun barrel had been jammed into his cheek.

107

'You know the drill,' said Hershey, her voice shrill and confused. 'Drop the gun and assume the position!'

'It's me, Hershey . . . Dredd,'

'I know who it is,' she hissed. 'Now drop the gun or I'll blow your drokking head off!'

'Cool down, Hershey! I'm on your side, remember,' he said, letting the Judge Pump fall to the ground. 'Look, I thought you were . . .'

'You thought I was what? Dead?' Hershey almost yelled. 'Thought, or hoped?'

'What happened?' asked Dredd, not daring to turn round in case Hershey had completely lost control.

'Someone tried to rearrange my living quarters with some hi-ex is what happened,' said Hershey. 'And if I hadn't been very lucky the next outfit I'd be measured for would've been a body bag!'

'How . . . ?'

'You tell me, Dredd . . . you tell me,' Hershey finally took the gun out his face and slumped against the wall. 'Over a hundred Judges have been killed in the last 48 hours . . . and this is the second time today I've nearly been trashed by a bomb.'

'Do you think I'm part of what's going on?'

'I don't know anything any more, Dredd.' Hershey shook her head. 'I don't even know who you really are.'

Something fell on the floor by Dredd's feet and he bent down to pick it up. It was the viewie of him and Rico at the Graduation Day celebrations all those long years ago.

'So tell me about him, Dredd.' Hershey walked out

108

of the bedroom, hardly glancing at Fergie. 'Make me believe in you like I did in that court-room.'

'His name is Rico.' Dredd turned and followed her out, staring at the picture in his hand. 'He's my ... my brother. He was the best Judge on the streets, the smartest, the most dedicated to upholding the Law ...' Dredd stopped talking.

'And?'

'And something happened to him, he went mad,' continued Dredd. 'He started saying Judges should rule, not serve – he became more dangerous than any criminal. A lot of people died trying to stop him, and I ended up having to judge him.'

'Is he responsible for this?' Hershey swung her arm around, indicating the trashed room: 'For everything that's going on out there?'

'Him,' nodded Dredd, 'and Griffin.'

'Griffin?' frowned Hershey. 'The Chief Justice? Do the Council Judges know?'

'The Council Judges are dead, Hershey.' Dredd gave her back the picture. 'Rico murdered them all, in cold blood.'

'We have to tell someone,' said Hershey. 'But I can't get through to Central because the console got fragged.'

'Er, 'scuse me for butting in,' Fergie said, rubbing his hands together, 'but this is where I think my particular, um, talents, might come in very useful.'

'Who's he?' asked Hershey.

'Ferguson, Herman Ferguson—'

'Call me Fergie.'

'He's a perp I was with on the Aspen Shuttle,' Dredd went on. 'I brought him back out of the Cursed Earth with me ... he's the guy I sent down for five after the Heavenly Haven incident, when Brisco got iced.'

'Unjustly sent me down,' corrected Fergie. 'You're reviewing my case, remember?'

'How could I forget,' said Dredd. 'So what is it you think you can do to be of use here?'

'Fix that terminal and patch you through to Central.'

'Well don't just stand there,' said Hershey, suddenly feeling very tired. 'Do it . . .'

Lights were burning bright in the Janus laboratory. The place had been completely cleaned and refitted with the equipment Griffin had stolen from Mega City Hospital. Chrome shone, glass sparkled and stainless steel glinted under the intense arc lamps, while under the watchful eye of the ABC Warrior, Rico waited by the main control console for Ilsa to join him.

'The DNA sample has been removed from its sub-zero cryo-chamber,' said Central, as Ilsa walked up. 'I am ready to start the cloning process.'

'Slight change of plan, Central,' smirked Rico. 'Purge that sample, I got a new one for you.'

'What on earth do you think you're doing, Rico?' demanded Ilsa.

'Activate DNA sampling device,' ordered Rico, ignoring her.

'Activated,' said Central, lights on the machine next to Rico flashing and blinking in a random pattern. It looked like a kind of mechanical scorpion.

Rico pulled his sleeve up and sat down; he put his arm in a special steel hollow and automatic clamps closed over it and locked. 'Central,' said Rico, 'take the sample – now!'

The tail of the scorpion-like machine shot down and the drill bit in. Its tip whirred as it stabbed Rico's arm, tiny flecks of blood spattering Ilsa Hayden's clothes.

'This was not part of our plan!' she said, angrily brushing them away. 'Judge Griffin never authorised us to—'

'It's not his job to authorise me to do anything.' Rico grabbed Ilsa with his other arm, making her gasp. 'I'm a free man now and no one tells me what to do, got that?'

'But Griffin's in control of this project,' exclaimed Ilsa, shaking herself free. 'It's his vision, he's the one trying to save Mega City!'

'He's a mental dwarf, just using *my* genius – and your talents, my dear – to give him power.' The sampling machine finished what it was doing and shut itself down, the tail rising and the clamps releasing Rico's arm. 'I'm in control now!'

'It was a mistake keeping you alive, Rico,' said Ilsa, rubbing her arm.

'But *I* am the future!'

'You,' Ilsa said slowly, moving away from him, 'are insane.'

'Don't give me that!' Rico wagged a finger at Ilsa as he followed her, backing her up into a corner so she couldn't get away. 'You didn't believe it when you said it at my trial, and you don't believe it now.'

'Why do you say that?' said Ilsa, looking Rico straight in the eyes.

'Because I think you know I'm right,' he replied, reaching up and patting her shoulder. 'And what's more I think you'd like to be a real part of what I'm doing.'

'Meaning?'

'Meaning, let's take some of *your* DNA,' Rico pointed at the sampling machine, 'and make some sugar and spice to go with the puppy dogs' tails . . .'

Chapter 16

In the rubbish tip that used to be Hershey's apartment Fergie was hunched over what was left of the console terminal. Printed circuit boards lay piled up beside him, tangled bundles of wires snaked everywhere and tiny silicon chips littered the desk top; Fergie was in seventh heaven.

There was nothing he liked more than being up to his armpits in the guts of a machine. He could do this kind of thing for hours and never get bored, and he didn't even mind doing it under pressure ... and he was certainly under pressure now.

Dredd and Hershey had left him to it and gone to sit in the bedroom. Both of them were dog-tired, every muscle in their bodies screaming for some rest; they sat next to each other on the bed, staring blankly at the wall.

'So, do you understand now?' asked Dredd.

'I understand why the DNA in the bullets that killed Hammond was the same as yours,' said Hershey. 'But I can't really believe it ...'

'Believe it.' Dredd got up and looked down at her. 'We're the same – clones, inhuman, defective clones – the only difference is, he went nuts before I did.'

'Cut it out, Dredd!'

'You said it yourself, Hershey ... I've got no friends, no feelings, no emotions ... I'm a machine, and a faulty one at that.'

'Dredd,' Hershey said gently, reaching out for his hand and taking it. 'The Janus Project didn't do that to you, you did it to yourself.'

Battered and exhausted as he was, Dredd could see the sense in what Hershey was saying; he squeezed her hand and was about to reply when Fergie walked into the bedroom.

'Oops, sorry guys! Didn't mean to spoil a Kodak moment ...' he said, turning round to go out again.

Dredd let Hershey's hand drop. 'What is it?'

'Well, I've fixed the microwave, but the terminal's another ball game entirely.'

'You can't mend it?' asked Hershey.

'I can't mend it completely,' shrugged Fergie. 'Too badly damaged for that, but I did manage to get it to dial out and access stuff.'

'What did you get?' demanded Hershey.

'Nothing. Zilch, zip and zero – I tried every database and node centre I could think of looking for that Janus thing,' said Fergie. 'I can't find it anywhere, not one sign.'

'Strange,' frowned Hershey. 'Though not impossible, considering the way Griffin's tried to keep it a secret ... but if it is back on line, Janus is going to need one heck of a lot of power.'

'Tried that angle as well,' nodded Fergie. 'There've been no recent applications for a new big-power user.'

'It's not going to be that simple.' Dredd massaged his chin as he thought. 'They wouldn't risk taking the kind of power they need straight out of the network ... somehow they're stealing it, hooking into various sources in one particular area.'

'But that would ...' said Fergie excitedly.

'Right,' Dredd nodded. 'That would cause blackouts and power surges – check every sector for anything like that in the last day or so.'

'Wait up!' Hershey pushed herself off the bed. 'Just before the mag-bomb took out my Lawmaster in Sector 4 there was a three-block-wide power surge, a big one ... didn't mean a thing to me at the time, but ...'

'I'm on to it, I'm on to it!' Fergie rushed back to the console. 'A power surge that big would leave a trail!'

'And could you follow it?' asked Dredd.

'Maybe,' said Fergie cautiously.

'You're such a genius, go do it,' said Hershey, and Dredd pointed back out of the room.

'That machine's half dead, guys!' said Fergie.

'Just do it, Ferguson.'

Fergie knew better than to argue. He went and sat at the keyboard to try and coax the terminal to do one last little thing for him. Information limped on to the screen agonisingly slowly, but at least, he thought, it was getting there.

'Here we go,' he said at last. 'I got the Sector 4 files for the day it happened ... here's some small overloads ... a spike ... and, yes! the big one! Now I got to put a tracer on it, and we'll have to wait.'

'How long will this take?' asked Dredd.

'As long as it takes,' grunted Fergie. 'This piece of junk's second cousin to a snail right now . . . here we go, though.' Fergie pointed to the screen and they all looked as a plan of the city appeared. Three blocks in Sector 4 were outlined in yellow and from them came a thin red line.

'What's happening?' said Hershey.

'The tracer's linking back to the source of the power surge,' explained Fergie. 'And from the look of it, it's going pretty deep.'

'They're hardly likely to be somewhere we can see them,' said Dredd.

'No need for sarcasm,' Fergie shot back. 'Something weird about the plans, though . . . I can't get this lump of garbage to change our point of view, but from the look of it there's something under that mess of buildings the trace has disappeared into.'

Hershey stood up. 'That's where they stuck the Statue of Liberty when it was moved it, ooh, seventy . . . eighty years ago.'

'I've seen that thing!' said Fergie. 'Stuff built all around it . . . looks kinda sad.'

'So they built their lab right beneath the Statue of Liberty.' Hershey looked over at Dredd.'

'Griffin's idea of a joke.' Dredd went to the bedroom and reappeared with his Judge Pump. 'I've got transport on the roof.'

'You won't be needing me any more,' grinned Fergie. 'So I'll say goodbye, then, OK?'

'Not OK,' said Dredd. 'You're coming with us.'

'Great,' sighed Fergie. 'More Judge Hunters, more pain, death and mayhem . . . just what I need . . .'

Griffin shut the door to the Janus Lab behind him. Across the room he could see Rico and Ilsa, heads almost touching as they bent down over a steel bench to look at something. They were talking quietly to each other, and didn't notice he'd come in.

The Chief Justice coughed. 'Dredd got away . . . the Hunters lost him.'

Rico stood up sharply and looked over his shoulder. 'Oh, it's you, Griffin . . . Don't get outta your pram, Chief – very shortly he's going to be seriously out-numbered, right Central?'

'Yes, Judge Rico,' said Central. 'The new DNA samples have been multi-plexed and the individual fused cells are already dividing.'

'New sample?' Griffin stopped half-way across the lab, next to the ABC Warrior. 'What do you mean – what's going on?'

'Look, that original DNA had been in the deep freeze over thirty years.' Rico shot an evil leer at Ilsa and she smiled back sweetly. 'Sooner or later you gotta clean out the fridge, know what I mean?'

'That sample was engineered to be the very best there was,' spluttered Griffin. 'What did you replace it with?'

Rico didn't say a word, just raised his eyebrows and showed Griffin his teeth.

'Oh my . . .' The Chief Justice put a hand to his face. 'You don't mean to say . . .'

'Congraulate me,' beamed Rico. 'I'm going to be the proud father of a drokking *platoon*, man!'

Griffin was dumbstruck. Everything he'd worked so

117

hard for was falling through his fingers like fine-grained sand. He watched open-mouthed as Rico went back to work.

'You . . . you don't know what you're doing!' he said. 'The sample has to be pure, free from any defects, or the accelerator will cause it to mutate – that's what happened the last time!'

'Must be why Dredd's such an ugly son-of-a-gun.'

'No! You don't understand – it was your DNA strand that was wrong, Rico!' Griffin was beginning to sound desperate. 'If you go and take copies of it it'll only make the mistakes even bigger – don't you see?'

Rico spun round, one of his hands knocking test tubes and scalpels on to the floor with a crash. 'You're *lying*!' he snarled. 'All you care about is power and control – well these Janus Judges won't listen to you, they'll be my children . . . my sons and daughters!'

'Daughters?' said Griffin, looking at Ilsa in disbelief. 'You're in this madness with him?'

'You've never fully understood the possibilities of Janus, Griffin.' She nodded at Rico. 'This project needs vision, not dumb management, and we can give it that, can't we, Rico?'

'Sure can, sweety,' said Rico, watching to see what Griffin would do next.

Foolishly he reached for his gun, but his hand had barely gripped its butt when the ABC Warrior clamped both his wrists and lifted him off the ground.

'You see, Griffin–' Rico seemed almost too calm under the circumstances – 'I'm not one of your typical, brainwashed Judges who do whatever they're told – I am a real man, I can think for myself ... and what I think is, you've had it, pal.'

Griffin struggled helplessly in the robot's iron clutches. 'Let me go – Central – do something!'

'I'm afraid the robot is not patched in to my control circuits, Chief Justice,' said Central. 'It's governed by a local command processor.'

'What?'

'Wise up, Griffin.' Rico walked over to stand near him. 'You can't expect to head up an outfit like the Justice Department if you don't understand the technology. The robot does what *I* say, and no one else.'

'Get it to put me down, Rico,' pleaded Griffin. 'I'm sure we can work this out to everyone's satisfaction.'

'Well I for one won't be satisfied until you are a distant memory, Chief.' Rico looked over Griffin's shoulder. 'Tear him apart, Fido ... slowly.'

'For Grud's sake!' screamed Griffin.

'Central,' said Rico, turning away, 'I think it's fair to say that the Chief Justice has just retired on the grounds of ill health ... and in his absence I have taken on all his responsibilities.'

The screams got louder and more frantic, and then stopped.

'He didn't even get to see his grandchildren,' said Rico. 'Shame ...'

Chapter 17

Dredd let Hershey and Fergie off the back of the Law-master and then hid it behind a large pile of rubble, the remains of a building trashed in the latest block war riot. All the lights down at street level had been broken, and only a hazy glow from the sprawl of high-rises, walkways and skyroads tried to cut the gloom.

Taking a hand-scanner off the bike, Dredd walked back to where Hershey and Fergie were waiting for him. He looked up as he made his way over the debris and could just make out the shadowy figure of what had once been a symbol of hope for everyone who came to the city. Somewhere up there the Statue of Liberty still held a torch for freedom, but now she was forgotten, caged in and trapped by a place that didn't understand the true meaning of the word.

'Let's find them.' Dredd gave Hershey the scanner and took his Judge Pump in both hands.

'Shall I stay here and guard the bike?' suggested Fergie.

'I'm going to need you.' Dredd motioned with the Pump for him to get moving. 'Someone's going to have to shut down the Janus system.'

'How did I know you were going to say that?' Fergie

sighed. 'I hate being right all the time, especially where you're concerned.'

'It's under this building,' said Hershey, looking at the scanner.

Dredd pulled back the safety catch on the Judge Pump – *KER-CHUNKK*! – The noise sounded unnaturally loud, like something biting metal. A shiver ran down Fergie's spine.

Hershey's torch beam lit up a door and Dredd kicked it open and went in. Fergie didn't want to follow, but he'd run out of choices. The building smelled old and disused, cobwebs hung in trails from the ceiling and unseen things skittered in the darkness. "Spooky" was hardly the word for the place.

'The power surge is this way,' said Hershey, pointing at some stairs that led even further below ground. At the end of the corridor torchlight picked out a pair of large steel doors. 'Wait a second . . . it's moving . . . that's not right . . .'

A shadow detached itself from the blackness and lunged at her. Hershey screamed as the ABC Warrior grabbed her and she dropped both the scanner and her Lawgiver.

'Look out!' Dredd yelled. The robot opened fire and its laser shot hit Fergie, sending him crashing against the wall.

'Knew I shoulda stayed in bed this morning,' he groaned.

There was a deafening crash and an explosion of light, and it was a couple of seconds before Fergie realised that Dredd had fired his Judge Pump at the robot. Curled up on the floor, he watched in amazement as Dredd and the ABC Warrior acted like a pair of Wild West cowboys from an old black-and-white vid show, advancing on each other, guns blazing.

For an insane few seconds the corridor roared with the sounds of death, Dredd's shells ricocheting off the robot's steel casing, while the robot, its aim worsened by Hershey's frantic struggling, sprayed fire all over the place. As Dredd got closer to the metal Warrior Fergie saw shreds of kevlar armour fly off his shoulder and then an electronic scream rang out.

'You got the son of a trash compacter!' yelled Fergie, wincing with pain as he saw the robot stop in its tracks, control cables in one of its legs shattered and oil pouring on to the concrete. Its damaged leg was shaking as if it was having a fit.

'Game over!' said a voice.

Fergie looked down the corridor and noticed that the steel doors had opened and two people – a man and a woman – were standing there, silhouetted by the bright lights of the room behind them. They were both holding guns.

'Drop the weapon, Dredd,' ordered the man.

'Get the tin can to let Hershey go.'

'I said drop the weapon,' repeated Rico. 'You got nothing to bargain with, Dredd. All I gotta do is tell Fido there to break her neck, and it's as good as done.'

'Hershey?'

'I'm OK, Dredd.' She looked at him. 'Really.'

Dredd let the Judge Pump slip from his hand and it fell beside Hershey's Lawgiver.

'How romantic, bro!' grinned Rico, watching Ilsa walk over to pick the weapons up. He could see Hershey and Dredd glance at each other, trying to work out if they could do anything. 'You got no chance, bro – now get your sorry self in the lab, and Fido ... if these two so much as burp, kill 'em!'

Pushing himself slowly up off the floor, Fergie saw Dredd walk slowly through the open doors. He could feel blood seeping out of his wound, and it throbbed with a hot, dull ache. 'Know what?' he said.

'No, what?' said Hershey quietly.

'This makes being nearly eaten by a bunch of psycho-cannibals look like a better deal ...'

'He looks like you,' said Ilsa, head on one side as she stood and observed Dredd.

'That's because he's just like me in so many ways,' Rico nodded to himself. 'Two peas out of the same test-tube pod, so to speak.'

'I'm nothing like you!' snarled Dredd, bunching his fists and for the first time feeling the pain in his shoulder where the robot had shot him.

'Wrong, wrong, wrong, bro!' laughed Rico. 'The only difference is, you destroyed your life for the sake of the Law ... and I am destroying the Law to create life. Look around you – *this* is the future!'

Dredd stopped staring at the person he now knew to be his brother and realised he was standing in a huge room. Hundreds of clear glass tubes seemed to be growing out of the floor, each one containing an unborn, mutant clone floating in a blue liquid. This

123

nightmare garden was lit by thousands of brilliant spotlights that seemed to make the pods glow.

'Welcome to the new world, same as the old world,' said Rico. 'Recognise it? This is where we were born, you and me!'

Dredd looked into one of the pods; the creature in it was almost fully grown and was turning slowly like it was asleep in bed. As he looked the creature opened its eyes and stared straight back, grinning. It was exactly like Rico, right down to the crazed smile.

'You've copied yourself...' whispered Dredd.

'Mass production, bro.'

Dredd tore his eyes away, feeling a sickness in his stomach that showed on his face.

'Don't look so *disappointed!*' said Rico. 'They ain't just me you know ... lotta you in there too, pal!'

'I don't need reminding,' said Dredd.

'You OK over there, Ferguson?' said Hershey, the robot's steel grip tight around her chest.

'I'm breathing, but I ain't dancing,' replied Fergie. 'How 'bout you?'

'Similar, Ferguson ... very similar.'

'What're we gonna do?'

'Not much I can do ... under the circumstances.'

'See your point,' said Fergie, edging forward to peer more closely at the robot. It was still standing stock still, pipes and cables splayed out from its damaged leg, oil dripping on to its foot.

'What are you doing?'

'Thinking,' said Fergie.

'Am I going to like what you're thinking?'

'I doubt it . . . cos I certainly don't . . .'

Chapter 18

Rico was at full speed and going into overdrive. He was striding up and down between the rows of growth pods, stroking the cool glass and looking for all the world like a proud father.

'Look, Joseph – my children!' he crowed. 'They'll be born in a few hours and I'll have an endless supply of perfect creatures just waiting on my every word. It was a choice, you see; either create a bunch of tin men with chips for brains and call them Judges, or go for the real thing!'

'You're sick, Rico.' Dredd couldn't bear to look at him. 'You couldn't even control yourself, back in the old days – what makes you think you can control these . . . these things now?'

Rico came over to stand near his brother. 'That's where you come in, Joe,' he said. 'I want to give you the chance to help, to join me in my brave new world.'

'I judged you once,' replied Dredd. 'I haven't changed my mind. You're a dead man, Rico, you just don't know it's over.'

'Now you mention it,' Rico came closer, 'all that time I spent racked up in that steel box in Aspen . . . I always wanted to know why.'

'Why what?'

'Why you judged me?'

'You killed innocent people, you caused a massacre and you betrayed the Law.' Dredd counted the points out on his fingers. 'Need I go on?'

'But you betrayed a friend, Joe,' Rico pouted. 'You talk to me about betrayal when you did that? We were brothers, even if we didn't know it back then, and now you gotta stick with me – us against them. You gotta stop being a slave and . . .' Rico paused.

'And what?'

'And choose, Joe. It's now or never.'

'You're going to have to kill me, Rico.' Dredd looked him in the eye.

'Why?'

'It's your only hope.'

'Fido!' Rico turned and yelled out of the doorway. 'Tear the nice Judge's arms and legs off, there's a good boy!'

'Don't, Rico!' Dredd stepped towards his brother.

'Back off, Joe,' said Rico. 'Fido, bring the little lady in here so's we can all say goodbye.'

'Rico.' Ilsa, who'd been watching her partner while she monitored the growth pods, came towards him. 'We've got work to do . . .'

'Stay away from me, Ilsa,' said Rico, his voice icy cold.

The robot limped into the room, dragging its bad leg on the floor. Hershey was gripped awkwardly in its arms, one hand behind her back, and there was something about her expression that made Dredd tense up. She didn't look like a person who was about to be ripped apart.

'OK.' Rico waved for the ABC Warrior to stop and it ground to a wheezing halt next to him. 'Do it.'

The robot turned its battered head to look around the room and then calmly dropped Hershey; as she fell to the floor it slammed its arm into Rico's chest and sent him flying backwards.

Ilsa screamed and ran over to him, but before she could get there the robot whirled round, picked her up and flung her across the lab. As it did so it turned its back to Dredd, who blinked in disbelief when he saw Fergie hanging on for dear life, his hands deep in the electronic innards.

'Dredd – catch!' shouted Hershey, throwing the Judge Pump she'd been hiding behind her back up to him. He caught it and turned to fire at Rico in one smooth move.

Rico dived out of the way, squeezing off a couple of shots at Dredd as he did so, and disappeared into the ranks of growth pods.

In the centre of the lab Fergie had lost control of the robot. It was crashing about the place, one arm trying to get rid of its unwanted passenger, its head jerking from side to side.

'No you don't, you jumped-up sardine can!' said Fergie, reaching in and pulling out a handful of coloured

128

wires. 'Once a hacker, always a hacker,' he grinned, tearing them apart.

The robot spasmed, throwing Fergie to the floor, a series of short-circuits blitzing through its wiring. Smoke began to pour out of every joint and the smell of fried chips and burning oil filled the air.

'Don't mess with the best,' groaned Fergie, watching the robot totter and slowly crash to the ground.

With Fergie and Dredd fully occupied, Hershey had gone to deal with Ilsa. She'd looked to be out for the count, but the moment Hershey bent over her she'd come back up fighting. The two of them fell at each other with jungle savagery.

A scattering of shots from Rico sent Dredd running for cover behind the fallen robot, where he discovered Fergie lying in a pool of blood.

'Hang on in there, Ferguson.' Dredd could see he looked bad. 'I'll be back to fix you up, soon as I've got Rico.'

'No time . . .' Fergie coughed, blood dribbling down his chin. 'You gotta say it, Dredd . . . before I go . . .'

Dredd frowned, and then realised what Fergie meant. 'I . . . I made a mistake,' he said. 'I'm sorry I misjudged you.'

'And you'll never arrest me again?'

'And I'll never arrest you again.'

'Too right, pal,' wheezed Fergie, grinning weakly, his eyes closing. 'I'm outta here . . . for good . . .'

'No!' Dredd almost yelled, gripping Fergie's wrist. 'Don't you dare . . .'

'RIIIIICO!!' screamed Dredd, standing up. He

reloaded his Judge Pump and charged towards the ranks of blue pods. He had only one thought in his mind, one face in front of him as a target for all his pain and grief. 'Rico, I'm coming to get you!'

Dredd fired at random, shells exploding into anything and everything. Hi-tech machinery was turned into so much junk metal, sparks flew and flames began to lick hungrily at spilt fluid.

Rico knew that it was only a matter of time before something hit him – and he knew he needed some help. Crawling through the wreckage towards the control console he was nearly whimpering with rage when he got there. All his dreams were cascading around him, and one man was responsible – he had to get Dredd!

'Central!' said Rico, a stray bullet whining above his head. 'Hatch the first set of clones immediately!'

'The cloning hasn't finished,' replied Central. 'The pod contents are only 60% complete—'

'Don't give me that!' interrupted Rico angrily. 'I need them now, so go ahead and start hatching!'

'As you wish, ah . . . Chief Judge,' said Central. 'But it is my duty to tell you that you may live to regret this decision.'

'I'm sure as heck gonna die it you don't get on with it!' said Rico.

Ilsa and Hershey were still locked in mortal combat –

all teeth and fists and nails, eye-gouging, hair-pull-
ing, anything-goes total mayhem.

'Got you!' grunted Hershey, hands gripped round
Ilsa's neck.

'Not yet!' Ilsa whacked a fist into Hershey's cheek
and rolled away, picking up a discarded wrench as
she did so. 'Eat this!' The wrench blow felled Hershey
and Ilsa kicked her as she stumbled forward.

Hershey didn't hit the ground. The fight had taken
them near to the growth pods, and she fell against
one of them. 'Oh my . . .' she said, her stomach heav-
ing. 'It's awake!'

In the pod, its weird, glassy eyes wide open, the
clone's mouth split open in a ripped grin. The level of
blue fluid was dropping rapidly.

'But . . . but it's not supposed to do this yet!' spluttered Ilsa, the wrench falling from her hand as she
stared at the pod.

'Well, believe me,' said Hershey as the pod opened
with a soft hiss, 'it surely is.'

Backing away, Hershey found herself next to Ilsa,
rooted to the spot at the sight of the half-formed clone
staggering out of the growth pod. For a moment Hershey didn't know whether to feel sorry for it or
disgusted by it; she settled for ignoring it and dealing
with Ilsa once and for all.

The lab was by now a disaster area of major proportions. Smoke hung from the ceiling almost to the floor
and Dredd had to run at a crouch to see where he was

going. And then, out of the blue, a hand grabbed his shoulder.

'Rico!' he said, turning. But it wasn't Rico, it was a partly formed half-man staring at him with Rico's eyes.

'Pain . . .' it croaked. 'P-A-I-N!'

'Cure!' said Dredd through gritted teeth, loosing off a shot. The creature's arms flung out sideways as it fell backwards and Dredd fired again, but this time – nothing. He was out of ammo in a room filling up with newly-birthed enemies.

All around him the lab was starting to shake, sparks showering out of the ceiling like miniature firework displays. Rico heard an insistent bleeping and looked down at his Lawgiver. A small red light was blinking on it.

'Ammo,' he muttered to himself. 'Low on ammo . . . must find Dredd.'

He moved out from behind the control console and was making his way across the floor when Dredd found him first, leaping out of nowhere and landing on his back. Rico's Lawgiver blasted shots wildly round the room, growth pods smashing, spilling their contents, which fell to the floor in a tangle of arms and legs.

The two men rolled over and over, tumbling down a short run of stairs with Dredd on top of Rico, pinning his arms to the ground as they landed.

'Grenade!' Rico yelled at his Lawgiver, pointing it round at Dredd.

'*All–lethal–rounds–finished* ... *select*?' said the gun's voice chip.

'Standard bullet!' screamed Rico, trying to stop Dredd inching the gun away from him.

'*All–lethal–rounds–finished* ... *select*?' repeated the gun.

'OK – smoke bomb, dammit!'

There was nothing Dredd could do. The round hit him in the chest like a sledgehammer and threw him up and over the railing to the bottom of the stairs, his shirt smoking.

'Central!' Rico stood up on shaky legs. 'Central, turn off all overhead lights!'

With only the floor lights to show the way, Rico pulled himself up the stairs and made a bee-line for the doorway.

Lying stunned on the floor, his chest soot-black from where the smoke bomb had hit him, Dredd eased himself up on to his elbows. It took a moment for him to realise that the ceiling lights had gone out.

'Central!' he shouted, and immediately started coughing. 'Turn the lights back on, Central!'

'Request denied,' said Central. 'Voice print confirms you to be escaped convict Joseph Dredd. You are advised to surrender to the authorities.'

Dredd was about to say something and then stopped for a second. 'OK, you win,' he said. 'I'll surrender to Judge Rico ... but I don't know where he is ...'

'That's not a problem,' replied Central helpfully. 'I have him on our scanners, he's up the stairs, straight

133

ahead and just outside the main doors. He appears to have activated the lift.'

'The lights, Central,' said Dredd. 'I can't find him in the dark.'

The overheads flickered on and Dredd hauled himself up the stairs. The lift would have to be the real way into the labs, he thought to himself, running through the smoke.

There was a dull *KRUUUMP*! behind him and he turned to see the command console explode in a sheet of flame. Hershey was still in there, somewhere, but he had to believe she could look after herself; if he didn't move fast Rico would get away, and he owed it to the man at his feet – and all the people who had died because of his madness – to stop him before he did any more permanent damage.

With a last look at Fergie, Dredd ran out into the corridor . . .

Chapter 19

He stood for a moment, trying to get his bearings, and then he saw it. A small red light glowing in dark. Dredd moved cautiously towards the glow and saw it was the lift's direction indicator – an arrow pointing upwards. Reaching out he punched the button below it and, after a few seconds' wait, the door slid open.

Dredd stepped inside, the door closing automatically behind him, and the lift started moving. It was only then he noticed there were no buttons on the inside; he was trapped, unable to control where he was being taken – but it must have been the same for Rico. And Rico had definitely been there. A bloody handprint on the wall showed where he'd steadied himself.

Dredd could feel the lift moving very fast; his stomach heaved slightly as it surged upwards. He felt guilty about leaving Hershey behind, but he had made a choice and there was nothing he could do about it now.

The lift suddenly slowed down and Dredd grabbed at the walls, just like Rico must have done shortly before him, and tensed, waiting for the door to open.

It slid back and a blast of cold, electrically-charged

air rushed in, and he took a deep breath, clearing his lungs of the stink of destruction, smoke and chaos from the underground labs.

Dredd slunk, panther-like, out of the lift. Lightning ripped the dark sky apart and a roll of thunder boomed over the city; he couldn't work out where he was for a moment, and then he didn't care because in front of him he saw Rico climbing on to a Mark IV Lawmaster. Silently Dredd tore across the gap between them and leapt at him as he started the bike up.

'No, Rico!' he yelled, slamming into him, and the two of them hit the ground. 'We've got some unfinished business, you and me!'

The riderless bike took off through an opening, stalled and then fell, tumbling, somersaulting, twisting its way to the ground below. In the sky above, the storm broke and a black, sooty rain began to fall. Dredd, who had landed on top of his brother, now realised where he was as a flash of sheet lightning illuminated the semi-circular room ... they were in the head of the Statue of Liberty.

The fall had made Rico drop his Lawgiver and the two men laid into each other with ferocious punches. When one landed on Dredd's wounded shoulder he lost his advantage and fell off Rico.

'This is how you repay me for telling you the truth!' Rico screamed, punching Dredd's shoulder again, and then dragging himself to his feet. 'I'm the only one who never lied to you, brother.'

Rico aimed a kick at Dredd. Rolling away from it he found himself slipping out of the Liberty Lady's crown . . . and then he was dangling in space, looking up at Rico.

'. . . I hereby judge you, Joseph Dredd.' Lightning flashed and Rico's eyes seemed to glow. 'And to the charge of betraying your one and only friend, I find you guilty!'

Rico bent down and picked up his Lawgiver. 'To the charge of betraying your own flesh and blood, I find you guilty!'

He put the gun to Dredd's face. 'And to the charge of being human when we both could have been so much more, *I–FIND–YOU–GUILTY*!' he screamed. 'And the sentence, is death!'

Rico pulled the trigger. Nothing happened.

'*All–lethal–rounds–finished . . . select?*'

Rico turned the gun and stared at it, furious he'd forgotten it wasn't working, and in that split second when he took his eyes off him, Dredd acted. Summoning up every last ounce of strength, he pulled himself up and grabbed the butt of the gun.

'*DNA–accepted . . . select?*'

'Signal flare!' yelled Dredd, pushing the gun round to point at Rico.

A violent ball of light shot past Rico's face, blinding him and making him stumble forward. As Dredd rolled himself away from the edge, Rico stepped into mid air and fell out of the crown.

'Got you!' Dredd's arm whipped out and caught his brother's wrist.

'You saved me, Joe?' Rico blinked up at Dredd. 'Why, bro?'

'Because you don't have to die.'

'I know that,' Rico grinned, suddenly reaching up and tearing Dredd's hand off his wrist. 'But you did give me a life sentence . . .'

There was nothing Dredd could do. Rico's hand slid from his and he fell out of his grip, sailed into the dark without a scream, and all Dredd was left with was the image of his brother's face grinning at him as the storm swallowed him up.

Chapter 20

He felt like an empty shell. In a matter of a few days he'd discovered a brother he never knew he had, and lost him forever. He put a hand down to push himself off the floor and a booted foot stepped on it. Hard.

Dredd looked up and saw Ilsa Hayden, clothes ripped and bloody, standing over him with the Judge Pump clutched in her blackened hands. One finger was curled round the trigger.

He closed his eyes as he saw the finger move and he heard a shot ring out. It wasn't the bear-like roar of an Judge Pump, but the harsh shout of a Lawgiver. Dredd opened his eyes to see Ilsa crumple in a heap on the floor next to him.

From the lift he made out Hershey coming towards him, smoke trailing from the barrel of her gun.

'Timing was always my strong point,' she said, reaching down to help him up.

'I had a feeling you'd make it, Hershey.'

'Lucky for you I did . . .'

They were supposed to be the upholders of the Law, to strike fear into the hearts of offenders everywhere.

139

What they looked like was a couple of people who'd looked Death in the face and only just managed to walk away.

Neither of them could speak. There was nothing left to say, except that they were alive and the ultimate threat to Mega City's future was dead. In front of them as they came out of the statue's base, Dredd saw the streets were filled with figures: fresh-faced Cadets, Judges on Lawmasters and heavily-armed Judge Hunters.

Lights – red, blue, white lights – flashed, their colours fading as the sun crawled over the skyline. The dawn of a new day.

'I thought it was all over,' Dredd looked away. 'But I guess I was wrong . . .'

A Judge Hunter broke ranks and came towards them.

'Am I under arrest?' Dredd asked him.

The Judge Hunter smiled. 'Not today, Judge Dredd . . . not today of all days. We know what Griffin was trying to do,' he said. 'We know you stopped him from making the Janus Project a reality.'

'Only just.' Dredd shook his head at the memory of how close the mad plan had come to actually working.

'We owe you a debt of gratitude, Dredd,' the Hunter carried on, 'and an apology for ever doubting your innocence.'

Dredd nodded. He wanted to smile but he was too tired.

'We have to reorganise the Council,' said the

Hunter. 'And it has been decided to offer you the position of Chief Justice . . . would you consider it?'

'It's an honour, but not one I can accept; I'm a street Judge, that's what I'm best at,' Dredd nodded towards Hershey. 'I recommend Judge Hershey.'

'What?'

'Would you take the post?' asked the Judge Hunter.

'I . . . I . . . are you sure?' she said, amazed at the suggestion.

'Don't be dumb, Hershey,' growled Dredd. 'It's what they call "a good career move". Take it.'

'I'd like to think about it, sir,' Hershey told the Hunter.

'Don't take too long,' said Dredd, turning to walk over to a Lawmaster that stood nearby, ready and waiting. 'If a Judge has to do anything, it's make quick decisions.'

'Wait!' called Hershey, running after him. 'We nearly die and you stroll off without even a goodbye?'

'Goodbye, Hershey.' Dredd reached for the helmet on the bike.

'Same old Dredd,' grinned Hershey, pausing then stretching up to kiss him.

'That's a Code 212: illegal physical contact with a Judge.'

'That's a load of garbage, Dredd.' She put her mouth to his ear and whispered. 'Feels good to be human, doesn't it?'

Dredd looked at her. 'I thought you'd say that.'

Dredd swung his leg over the Lawmaster's saddle.

Sitting back he relaxed and finally allowed himself to smile. Then he started up the bike.

The roar of the engine echoed off the buildings. The crowds cheered.

It felt good to be alive.

It felt better to be back on the streets.